Praise for the Grime Solver's Myst̲e̲ri̲e̲s

"[A] charming, ̲nse
whodunit that su̲b̲ ̲ ̲ ̲ ̲ ̲ ̲ ̲ ̲ ̲ ̲ ̲ ̲ ̲ ̲ ̲ ̲ ̲ ̲ ̲ette

Sc̲e̲n̲e̲ o̲f̲ t̲h̲e̲ Grime
"[A] delightful, sassy tale filled with eccentric, interesting characters that add to the whodunit."

—The Best Reviews

"The first Grime Solvers Mystery, introducing cleaning expert Sky Taylor, has lots of promise—an interesting main character, a charming Massachusetts town with plenty of secrets, and several possible love interests for Sky. Readers will enjoy getting to know Sky and the people of Pigeon Cove. Several great cleaning tips are also included." —*Romantic Times*

"*Scene of the Grime* is a well-written, fun, delightful novel. The characters are vividly drawn and the dialogue sparkles. . . . I very much enjoyed reading this book and look forward to the next Grime Solvers Mystery." —MyShelf.com

"[A] light, enjoyable read—and the cleaning tips [are] spot on." —Gumshoe

Also by Suzanne Price

Dirty Deeds
Scene of the Grime

NOTORIOUSLY NEAT

· A GRIME SOLVERS MYSTERY

Suzanne Price

AN OBSIDIAN MYSTERY

OBSIDIAN
Published by New American Library, a division of
Penguin Group (USA) Inc., 375 Hudson Street,
New York, New York 10014, USA
Penguin Group (Canada), 90 Eglinton Avenue East, Suite 700, Toronto,
Ontario M4P 2Y3, Canada (a division of Pearson Penguin Canada Inc.)
Penguin Books Ltd., 80 Strand, London WC2R 0RL, England
Penguin Ireland, 25 St. Stephen's Green, Dublin 2,
Ireland (a division of Penguin Books Ltd.)
Penguin Group (Australia), 250 Camberwell Road, Camberwell, Victoria 3124,
Australia (a division of Pearson Australia Group Pty. Ltd.)
Penguin Books India Pvt. Ltd., 11 Community Centre, Panchsheel Park,
New Delhi - 110 017, India
Penguin Group (NZ), 67 Apollo Drive, Rosedale, North Shore 0632,
New Zealand (a division of Pearson New Zealand Ltd.)
Penguin Books (South Africa) (Pty.) Ltd., 24 Sturdee Avenue,
Rosebank, Johannesburg 2196, South Africa

Penguin Books Ltd., Registered Offices:
80 Strand, London WC2R 0RL, England

First published by Obsidian, an imprint of New American Library,
a division of Penguin Group (USA) Inc.

First Printing, April 2009
10 9 8 7 6 5 4 3 2 1

In loving memory of Noni Kosinski.
An angel while here, now on the other side.

Acknowledgments

Thanks to our good friend Will Weiss for his indispensable proofreading of the Spanish dialogue in this book. We'd hate to think what Sky and Orlando would have done—or *said* to each other—without him.

Helping Hands: Monkey Helpers for the Disabled is an actual nonprofit organization serving quadriplegics and other people with severe spinal cord injuries or mobility impairments. Based in Boston, it provides highly trained capuchin monkeys to assist with daily activities. Those who wish to learn more about this fantastic program may do so at its official Web site, www.monkeyhelpers.org.

A tip of the broom goes to our agent, John Talbot, for his professional guidance and advice, and most of all for his friendship.

Our editor, Kristen Weber, has definitely earned the Golden Spray Bottle Award—or *some* kind of award, anyway—for patience above and beyond the call of duty. Her enthusiasm and gentle hand in shepherding this series along is deeply appreciated.

Finally, the Grime Solvers novels owe a great deal to the humor, wisdom, and kindness of Suzanne's late mother, Noni Kosinski, who was endlessly providing us with new cleaning tips for these books, and loved them more than any we've written. Noni was reading an advance copy of the previous entry in the series, *Dirty Deeds*, when she unexpectedly left us. Of the loss of a mother, a good friend said, "There's before and there's after, and every day for the rest of your life is after." Nothing could be truer.

We honor her as best we can by moving forward with optimism and determination.

Chapter 1

Spring had arrived in the town of Pigeon Cove. Well, spring with an asterisk. The snow was gone, the grass was green, and tulips lined our garden paths like cups of brightly colored paint.

It was cold, though. Not just sort of. It was c-c-*cold*. The coldest spring Covers could remember.

That's why the shivery asterisk, if you're wondering. Since moving to New England, I'd found out that overcoat weather could stick around until the Fourth of July or so.

Still, I was primed for the new season despite a lingering case of the sniffles. This was partly because I was also good to go for my first official romantic date with dashing police chief Alejandro Vega—or Alex, as he kept asking me to call him—with not a thought in my mind about Mike Ennis.

Okay. Let's add another of those pesky, clingy little asterisks to the word "not."

But I'll get to Mike in a while.

Mike wasn't *now*.

Now, with hesitant spring and tentative romance in the wishfully seasonable air, I, Sky Taylor, was pretty darned ready for dinner and whatever might happen afterward with Chief—um, Alex.

And if it sounds like I was indecisive . . . I can tell you I was very open to persuasion about the *afterward* part. I know how quickly things can be taken away from us, and that's taught me to live life to its fullest.

More on that later too.

Happily, I'd found my sexy but too-light-for-the-weather clothes the slightest bit loose as I'd put together my outfit for the evening. Thanks to hours of self-inflicted torture at the Get Thinner gym, I was at my all-time slimmest despite a winter of noshing on hearty stews, creamy chowders, and sugary cakes and muffins—making me feel downright glamorous in a pair of skinny black pants, high-heeled chocolate ankle boots, and my mother's latest fashion concept, the so-called kite tunic.

If you haven't caught on to Betty's new chicychic, retro, hippie-dippie designer-clothes Web site, I should explain that her tunic—item number five on her e-catalog's "Asian Vibrations" page—was actually a tapered tuxedo shirt dyed pink and then hand painted with dozens of pastel origami-type cranes flying through the air. And while I'm explaining things, I might as well mention that there was a special reason for my Japanese-inspired style that evening. This being that Chief Al and I were having dinner at a Japanese restaurant.

It wasn't just your average old sushi bar.

An old waterfront manor renovated in the style of a traditional Japanese home—known as a *minka*—Shoko's Minka was the most popular new eatery on the North Shore. Though the food was scrumptious, its atmosphere was responsible for a lot of the hoo-ha about it, and made up a big reason there were no open reservations till Saint Swithin's Day . . . unless you happened to be the police chief or some other local VIP.

Of course, going out for Japanese is never just about the meal. Or shouldn't be. It's about an aesthetic too—doing more with less to maintain the balance of nature's beauty. At Shoko's, with its spacious interior and mix of low traditional tables and American-style teakwood table and chair

3

sets, diffuse lighting through rice paper shoji doors blurred the lines between the dining room and the landscaped garden outside.

The chief—that's to say, Alex—had arranged to have one of the traditional tables set aside for us, thinking we should have the total experience. But when our lavish, delicacy-filled bento boxes arrived, he seemed mildly worried about his choice.

"You're sure you think it's comfortable on this mat?" he said, patting the tatami underneath him. "If you'd rather have a chair, I'll ask for a regular table."

"This is wonderful. I wouldn't want to be anywhere else," I said, which was absolutely true. In fact, I'd never known there'd be a hibachi built right into the table to keep us toasty warm even with the patio door open.

I dabbed a seaweed-wrapped rice ball with some wasabi, popped it into my mouth, and devoured it. Chief Alex, meanwhile, looked as if I'd only partially eased his concern.

"How about your leg?" he said. "It's okay now? I mean, okay enough for us to sit on the floor like this?"

"The leg's been fine for ages." I resisted the urge to do a demonstrative knee flex and show I was fully rehabbed after the Christmas whacking

I'd gotten from a drunken fisherman. "Bry deserves serious credit."

"The kid who came to the rescue when you were attacked?"

"Bryan Dermond, right."

"Doesn't he handle the Internet stuff for the newspaper?"

"Used to," I said. "He went full-time as my assistant two, three weeks ago."

"Ah-hah." Vega nodded. "That explains why he's been answering the phone at your new office . . ."

"Answers the phone, manages my Web site, and handles some of my more physical cleaning jobs. You name it. Thanks to Bry, I can take things a little easier these days."

That was also the unadulterated truth. My sweet but frightfully pierced and studded sidekick had turned out to be a *huge* help, proving to be as creative as he was reliable, especially when it came to using fewer chemical cleaning products in his effort to go green, something he'd likewise convinced me to do.

Chief Alex picked up a shrimp with his chopsticks. My own chopsticks swooped at the *negimaki*, a grilled beef–and-scallion roll I'd been eyeing since the waitress brought our meal. I'd wanted to hold off on it till the red-hot wasabi cleared my stuffy nose—and restored my sense of taste so I could appreciate the morsel's delicate flavors.

It was well on its way into my mouth when I heard a loud commotion from over by the patio across the dining floor to my right and—

Wait. Whoa. Strike that.

To call what happened a "commotion" is an understatement verging on the ridiculous.

The word doesn't come close to describing the shrill screams of confused, horrified diners and servers, the loud crash of chairs and dinnerware, or the simultaneous and totally freak-out-worthy chorus of barks, grunts, neighs, and squawks that accompanied the rest of that bestial cacophony.

I'll mention the hoofbeats later. This is mainly because my brain was on a ten-second time delay as far as realizing what they were. But it's also because I should probably talk about the monkey first.

The monkey was what jolted me out of my utter shock and disbelief as it plucked the *negimaki* from my chopsticks, bit off half of it with a smack of its rubbery lips, and then generously held the rest out to me in a furry, almost human paw.

Now, I will admit it was a cute monkey. A very, very cute brown monkey. Not that I've ever been aware of *un*cute ones. This particular primate, however, was only a little over a foot tall, weighed five pounds tops, and had a wrinkled round face under a high tuft of fur that resembled a radical fifties pompadour and was several shades darker than the rest of its fur. Its twinkling almond eyes said it probably enjoyed a good laugh every so often—and I would find out later that it did. I'd also learn that it was a trained capuchin named Mickey who knew how to prepare microwavable popcorn, could operate a DVD player, and really would have preferred a peanut butter–cucumber sandwich, or maybe a handful of Tic Tacs, to a stolen rice ball.

But later's for later. Since I already have to explain all about Mike and me, we'll just add Mickey to the list. Their names are alphabetically proximate anyway.

There at Shoko's Madhouse, I wanted only to pull myself together and figure out what in the world was going on as the creature—who'd seemingly taken my befuddled stare as a no-thanks to its offer to share the bento box delicacy I'd thought was mine—gulped down what was left of it, let out a contented grunt, and sprang from the table to my lap with a kind of soft, fur-butted thud. Before I could react, it had scrambled up my body and wrapped its scrawny monkey arms tightly around my neck.

"Chief Vega!" I hollered, unable to even blame myself for reverting to the formalese under the circumstances. "It's a monkey! We've got a monkey at our ta—"

Then I cut myself off. Not because I was dumb enough to think the chief wouldn't have noticed the fuzzy little thing giving me a hug. But because I'd suddenly realized Vega had leaped up to his feet from the tatami and was staring gape-eyed at the very large and diverse menagerie of critters charging in our direction—and every other direction besides, racing round and round the room in a chaotic frenzy.

As I also got to my feet, my shrieking, grinning, food-grabbing simian pal still wrapped affectionately around me, a greyhound came springing through the patio door behind a pony or miniature horse—not being Jack Hanna or Dr. Dolittle, I didn't know which it was. But its hooves were clopping and clomping pretty loudly as the dog ran into a tiny kimono-clad waitress, knocking her to the floor, saki glass–laden tray and all.

Sprawled on her back among the spilled drinks, she shouted something that sounded like *"Hidee-na!"*

I didn't know what that meant. But it sounded panicked. Justifiably.

This is what I remember of the next minute or two's confusion:

The horsey-pony thing galloping past the waitress and knocking over a cabinet full of china. An alpaca—that's right, *alpaca*—spitting in the teacups of mortified customers I recognized as Rena and Ritchie Freund, the saltwater-taffy makers. Dishes crashing to the floor as maybe a dozen cats pounced and skidded across tabletops. Chairs toppling over as a honking white goose harassed Henry Stootz, the hairdresser. And then the vegetable man Gazi Del Turko's little girls, Evie and Persha, squealing with sheer delight as a peacock strolled into the place behind the rest of the zoo crew, regally unfanning a large plume of iridescent blue tail feathers.

When the police came dashing into the restaurant behind the stampede, it was oddly anticlimactic. Well, I shouldn't speak for everybody. Although the waitress with the saki tray had collected herself, a cashier with a phone in her hand was still screaming her lungs out in Japanese.

For the record, the word she was hollering was *"Omawari!"*

Which I later learned, but will tell you right this instant, meant "Cops!" Not wanting to make you wait for everything.

And then one of the officers—it was my old square-jawed friend Ronnie Connors—pulled to a halt in front of us.

"Chief Vega," he began breathlessly, pausing an incredulous beat to notice the huggy monkey in my arms. "Chief . . . it's the veterinarian across the road. Someone's murdered her."

I squeezed Mickey, who I did not yet know was named Mickey, as tightly as I could.

"Dr. Pilsner?" I said with horror. *"Gail* Pilsner?"

I felt my spine stiffen. Alex looked at me. I looked at him. And then we both stood there at a loss for words as something soft and downy quacked between my ankles.

Gail Pilsner was my cat Skiball's vet and every pet owner in town's favorite animal doc. Besides being smart, experienced, and compassionate, she was the only one around to specialize in exotic creatures like monkeys and alpacas.

She was also one of my cleaning accounts. Bry's weekly cleanup of her offices and boarding kennels had inspired him to post some pet-cleaning hints on our Web site's Grime Solvers blog.

I obviously knew Gail's office was across the road. I had also seen a pack of escaped animals invade the restaurant, and heard a very distressed uniformed officer say the word "murder" in connection to the reason for their escape. That made my question to him the very definition of rhetorical. Of course he'd meant Dr. Pilsner. Who *else* would it have been?

I squeezed my new monkey friend against my chest for comfort, and listened to Connors continue to fill in Chief Vega.

"... think we have a suspect," he was in the middle of saying. "Caught him trying to make tracks. It's the kid who works there ... He's talking a mile a minute in Spanish and we need you to translate."

A second passed. Dr. Pilsner's kennel assistant, Orlando, was a Dominican immigrant who barely spoke a word of English. But he'd always seemed very sweet, and Gail had adored him—I must have heard her mention how gentle he was with the animals a dozen times.

I sat there looking stunned. It was hard to imagine Orlando hurting anyone, let alone her.

Then Chief Vega said, "I don't speak a word of Spanish."

Connors looked at him, mystified.

"But I figured—"

"My father came from Mexico," Vega said. "That doesn't mean I speak Spanish. Any more than my mother being Irish American gives me a brogue."

Although it did explain his sexy emerald green eyes, I thought but didn't say.

Connors had flushed with embarrassment.

"Oh," he said.

"Right," Vega said.

"But we need somebody who—"

"I speak it," I said, breaking a hand free from the monkey's hug to wave it in the air. "Fluently."

The two men looked at me.

"You do?" asked Vega.

"College minor—and I lived in New York," I said with a nod.

He looked at me for a moment. The monkey reached for my upraised hand, tugged it down by the wrist, and pressed my palm against the top of its head, making an improvised monkey cap out of it.

Then we heard a terrific bang somewhere in the restaurant, followed by an exclamation that I'd phonetically approximate as, *"Gua-ooo-laaah!"* I think it was bestial in origin, but it might have been a person who was really upset.

Chief Vega grabbed my elbow and started toward the patio door.

"We'd better hurry up," he said.

I hurried.

Its cheek pressing against mine, my monkey pal hung on for the ride.

SKY TAYLOR'S GRIME SOLVERS BLOG

Bry the Wonder Guy's Awesomely Cool Cleaning Tips for Pet Owners

When it comes to cleaning, Sky's the Limit and I'm not. But it ain't like I totally *bite*—I mean, Skyster never would've made me her apprentice if I didn't have the clean gene in my cells. Or somewhere. Anyway, I cooked up these hints for pet owners, and now she says I gotta be a sharer. So check 'em out. You'll stress less over Cuddles's next mess.

1. Fleas were put on this world for a single, solitary reason, namely, teaching us how to hate living things that're way smaller than

we are. My advice is to keep your carpet flea free, since that's where they lie low waiting to hop aboard the Cuddles Express.

The best way to obliterate 'em is with old-school mothballs. Pop a couple into your vacuum cleaner bag before turning on the machine. Then go ahead and vacuum. Most of the fleas you suck up are gonna be instant toast—and the rest are gonna wish they were. When you're done vacuuming, take the bag out of the vac right away, close it up in a plastic bag, and trash it. *Sayonara*, bloodsuckers.

2. Listen to me, ppl, litter ain't just for cats. Say your dog has an overshare moment in the house—i.e., goes poopsie-doopsie on the rug. You can either stand there screaming, *"Urgent!"* or deal with it. Pouring cat litter on the mess makes pickup a snap by drying some of the moisture and . . . well, I don't hafta get any more graphic. Try it. Nobody sez you'll like it. But you'll wanna thank me once you quit holding your nose.

3. While we're on the subject of accidents, here's a tip for when Cuddles leaves a pud-

dle on a concrete floor—say in your garage or basement. Kinda like what golfers call a water hazard, except for your foot instead of a ball. To zap the *eau de urine*, soak the floor with equal parts vinegar and water. That'll also keep your furry little bud from coming back to that spot to do its business.

4. Y'know that cheapo grooming brush you bought and never use? The rubbery one that pulls Cuddles's fur, and makes him stare at you like you're some freaked-out dom chick whenever it comes out of the drawer? I suggest you resist the urge to chuck it in the trash, since it's good for getting pet fur off upholstered chairs and couches. Run it over the cushions and it'll clump the fur for easy pickup. Big plus: Unlike your dog or cat, the couch won't nip, scratch, or scram into the next room.

5. Don't get caught without a pickup bag when walking your dog—unless you're into paying fines and getting the one-finger howdy from poop-phobe neighbors. I buy small black scooper bags at the pet shop, take a few out of the pack, fold 'em lengthwise, and

tie them to the handle of my dog Tat's (yeah, that's short for Tattoo) retractable leash. Usually I put about four of them on for starters. Since I hang the collar and leash on a coat hook near the door, I can't miss noticing when I'm down to the last bag. That's when I substitute new ones for the bags I've used.

While I'm talkin' retractable-leash utility: I know people in the Cove never lock their doors, but it ain't so in Gloucester, where my apartment door's got a spring lock that bolts on its own. If yours does too, I've got some advice. Put a spare house key in some plastic wrap, lay it flat against the side of the leash handle, and then wind some duct tape around it. If you've got an inner and outer door, use both sides of the handle, one for each key. The plastic keeps the tape from gumming up your keys. Some night when Cuddles drags you out of bed on an emergency run, you'll realize you forgot your keys and be glad I kept you from freezing to death in your pj's.

6. One for the birds, ha-ha. Spread a layer of wax or parchment paper on the bottom before you line the cage with newspaper. How

come? you ask. 'Cause it keeps the newspaper from sticking to the bottom of the cage after Pretty Boy does his thing (and does it and does it and does it, if you know what I'm sayin'). Besides that, it makes scraping history. Spray the cage bottom with pet-safe cleaner and wipe dry. Done.

7. Final words: Be effective, not defective. And, uh . . . later for monkey tips, sisses and bros.

Chapter 2

Dr. Gail Pilsner's veterinary clinic and pet-boarding kennels were on the first floor of an expansive three-story Colonial that doubled as her home.

As I went rushing over with the two policemen and the clingy brown monkey, I saw an EMS vehicle from Addison Gilbert Hospital parked out front behind a couple of patrol cars and the coroner's station wagon. To my surprise, Corinne Blodgett from City Hall stood out front talking to an officer with a notepad, her yappy little Lhasa apso running tangled circles around her legs on an extendable leash. But I was too busy breathlessly keeping up with Vega to wonder what Corinne was doing there.

Dr. Pilsner's residential entrance was beyond

the vehicles at the curb, set slightly back on a low hill with a half dozen wooden steps climbing to the top. She had used a door at the side of her house for her veterinary practice, where yet another cruiser sat with its roof hurling off strobes of red and blue light. Sawhorses had been hastily thrown up in the cross streets to detour traffic away from the place.

"We got the assistant in the kennel," Connors said, hustling along between Vega and me. "The body's in the front foyer . . . at the bottom of the stairs."

Vega glanced over at him.

"You're sure this wasn't an accident?"

"No way," Connors said. "She went clear through the rail."

Vega picked up his pace. It was somehow odd to see him acting every bit the top cop in his dress clothes, racing along in an expensive charcoal suit, his necktie flapping in the wind. "I want to have a look. Bring Sky around to the clinic and wait for m—"

"Hey, Chief!"

Vega looked uphill to where another of his cops stood looking down at us.

"What is it?"

"Those EMS guys are making a fuss." The cop

jabbed a thumb back over his shoulder. "They claim they're in some kind of hurry."

Vega put on a sudden burst of speed. He reached the sidewalk, took the steps leading uphill two at a time, and disappeared into the house.

I tried to stay close on his heels. Although I couldn't have explained why, not at that moment, I couldn't resist the urge to see what had happened with my own eyes.

"Whoa . . . hold on, miss!" Connors said from behind me. I'd reached the bottom of the wooden steps. "We're supposed to be going—"

I knew where we were supposed to be going, and didn't care. Rushing up the steps, I followed Vega through the entrance—and almost crashed into a pair of white-uniformed emergency technicians standing just inside the vestibule.

Both turned to face me as I came to a halt. I was back to feeling congested—with the sinus-opening wasabi having worn off, the dash from Shoko's Minka left me gasping for breath.

"You again," one of them said with a frown.

"*Her* again." The other scowled.

I recognized them immediately. The first guy was named Hibbard. The other was named Hornby. Hibbard had brown hair, Hornby blond. Hibbard was about fifty and pudgy, Hornby thirtyish and thinner. Hibbard was a certified paramedic, while Hornby's training qualified him only as a basic emergency tech. The men would often insist on pointing out there was a difference, a para being able to administer injections, IV drips, and the like to a patient, whereas a tech couldn't legally stick a needle in anyone. It seemed to me that Hornby deferred to and admired his older partner, possibly hoping to someday rack up the hours and test scores needed to attain his specialized rating.

"Me again, right," I said, wondering why they seemed so unhappy with my arrival. "Is something wrong with that?"

"Nope," said Hibbard.

"Not a thing," stressed Hornby.

"Except," Hibbard said, glancing at his partner.

Hornby returned the look and nodded.

I stared at the mellifluously paired EMTs. "Except what?"

Hibbard hesitated but didn't say anything.

"What?" I repeated.

The para was silent another moment. Then his eyes abruptly grew large. "Hey!" he said. "There's an animal hanging on to you."

"It took you *this* long to notice?"

"Don't pull his leg," Hornby said. "He's serious."

"I'm not pulling anybody's leg. Of course there's an animal hanging on to me."

"Is it a baby chimpanzee?" said Hornby.

"Or a possum?" said Hibbard.

"How about a koala? I heard koalas have strong grips like this one's got."

"He's a monkey." I tried to look past the EMTs toward the staircase, but they were standing right in my line of sight. "Now would you two please excuse me . . . ?"

"I don't know," Hornby persisted. "That thing looks to me like one of those Aussie marsupials I saw on the National Geographic Channel. Like maybe a wombat. Or a kangaroo, I'm not sure which . . ."

"I told you, he's a monkey," I said impatiently. "How in the world can you two not tell he's a monkey?"

"Before you get started on that, how can *you* tell it's a 'he' and not a 'she'?"

I looked at him.

"You'd kind of have to be blind not to know," I said. "It isn't as if he's wearing monkey pants."

The techs stared at me. Okay, make that stared at "us." Me and my monkey friend, I mean. I hitched him defensively up in my arms.

"Look, you don't have to get snippy," Hornby

said. "We're emergency responders for when humans get in trouble, not veterinary techs."

"Meaning we can't identify every single creature in the animal kingdom," Hibbard said.

"Which, come to think, the victim probably could've done if she wasn't deceased . . ."

"Something we can officially state is her present condition, being that a coroner's assistant accompanied us to the scene this time. As opposed to *last time* we were all together under similar circumstances," Hibbard said. His eyes beaded on me. "Or the time before that. When Dr. Maji didn't have an assistant to send along with us. Which he does now, probably because we've had a big spike in suspicious deaths since a certain somebody came to the Cove."

Hibbard and Hornby went back to exchanging meaningful glances. We'd had two murders—and maybe three now—in town since I moved up from New York. There was poor Abe Monahan at the Millwood Inn last spring, and then Kyle Fipps at the Art Association's Christmas party. The common thread being that I'd just so happened to be the person who stumbled on the bodies. Well, okay, I shared the ghastly honors with my best friend, Chloe, when it came to finding Kyle. The thing was, though, that I didn't like what Hibbard had implied any more than I appreciated the looks he kept swapping with his pal.

"Are you saying I'm some kind of *jinx*?" I asked.

The EMTs shifted uncomfortably on their feet.

"You hear anybody use that word?" Hibbard replied. "I know I didn't use that word."

"But say he would've used it. He might have also pointed out that you're two for two so far . . . three for three if you want to count the present occasion," Hornby said. "Not that either of us believes in jinxes. As technical personnel we aren't superstitious types."

I stared at him. The monkey reached a finger up and strummed my lower lip. I pulled his hand, or paw, or whatever it was, away from my face so I wouldn't blubber.

"If it wasn't too idiotic to even discuss, *I* could point out that you both showed up ahead of me tonight," I said. "But I won't. Considering there are more important things going on."

They seemed taken aback.

"There you go getting touchy again," Hibbard said.

"We're just trying to do our job," Hornby said.

"Something you might want to explain to your, uh, good friend Chief Vega, since his officers seem clueless about what that job happens to be."

That was enough for me. I'd had it with those two big galoots.

I frowned and pushed past them into the hallway.

Seeing Dr. Pilsner's body near the foot of the stairs came as a huge shock. It didn't matter that I'd expected it. There was no way to avoid being shocked when you saw someone who'd been full of vitality with his or her life suddenly and prematurely snuffed out. And when a life was snuffed out by what looked to be a terrible, vicious act, the insult to the senses seemed all the worse.

Gail Pilsner had handled the creatures entrusted to her care with a gentle kindness that made her the most popular vet in town, endearing her even to people who weren't animal lovers or pet owners. But it was clear at once that there was nothing kind or gentle about how she'd met her end. She lay in a heap amid broken, splintered pieces of the banister, wearing a lab coat that had been partially torn off to reveal the plain plaid blouse and khaki slacks she had on underneath.

Bent into unnatural positions, her outspread arms and legs looked almost boneless—but, of course, I knew that just meant a great many of Gail's bones had been shattered.

As shattered as the rail and spindles that had gone crashing from the stairs to the floor with her.

I emerged from between Hibbard and Hornby to find the new assistant coroner crouched over the body, a suitcase-sized metal crime-scene kit open on the floor beside her. A slim woman in her mid-thirties with narrow black-rimmed eyeglasses and blond hair pulled severely back from her face, Liz Delman had been working under Dr. Maji for a couple of months now. Though she'd bought a saltbox home not far from the Fog Bell Inn, where I was staying on with Chloe and her husband, I hadn't gotten to know her too well . . . and neither had anyone else in the Cove. Liz mostly ignored people and seemed almost motorized in the way she'd hurry past you on the street.

"She's only been dead a short time," she said to Chief Vega and two or three other officers standing around her. "My estimate would be less than an hour."

"Any ideas about the COD?" Vega said. In police jargon that was short for "cause of death." Though I don't suppose anyone would have confused it with "cash on delivery" given the circumstances.

Liz was packing away her equipment. "There's serious damage to the C-three vertebra."

"A broken neck," Vega said.

"In layman's terms, yes."

"You think it happened before she went through the rail? Or as a result of the fall?"

"I don't do instant reports, Chief," she said curtly. "That's why we conduct autopsies at the hospital."

Vega watched Liz latch her kit shut and rise to her feet. I didn't think he appreciated her condescending attitude. But I also didn't think he intended to call her out on it . . . not at that very inappropriate point in time.

The two EMTs chimed in before I could find out for sure.

"This is exactly what we've been telling your boys, Chief," Hibbard said. "Thanks to the assistant coroner, we can state for the record that we have a deceased, nonresuscitable person here."

"Meaning there's no sense in us hanging around," Hornby said. "If it's all the same to you, we'd like to load her up in the wagon and be on our way—"

Vega cut him short with a glance. He seemed

ticked, putting it politely. "A woman's been killed. As of right now this is a crime scene," he said. "You'll wait till I'm finished inspecting it and collecting evidence."

In fairness to the techs, I thought they looked sort of contrite. They went back to shuffling their feet, finally stepping aside as Liz Delman shouldered past them to the door.

Vega quietly studied the broken handrail. After what seemed a long while, he turned to an officer who'd been in the hallway with Liz when we arrived.

"It would've taken a lot to send her clear through that rail," Vega said. "A whole lot."

I could guess what he was thinking. Gail was five six or so and weighed maybe 110 pounds. A woman that petite wouldn't have taken down what appeared to be a solid mahogany banister unless she was pushed hard—and with very deliberate intent.

Vega kept looking at the cop, a young rookie with a dimpled baby face—I swear he could have been mistaken for a high school kid—named Jerred. And in case you're wondering, I knew he was a rookie from a story my kinda sorta ex Mike Ennis had written in the *Anchor* introducing him to the town's residents.

"You answered the nine-eleven?"

"Right," Jerred said. "With Connors."

"I don't remember you being on tonight's duty roster."

"I wasn't, Chief. But Elroy called in sick and I offered to cover for him."

Vega rubbed the back of his neck. This was something he did when he was thinking hard. "Who found the body?"

"The woman outside giving a statement," Jerred said. "She's got that little shaggy dog . . ."

"Her name is Corinne Blodgett," I said. "I think her dog is Zsa Zsa."

Vega faced me abruptly. I could tell he was surprised to hear my voice, and realized he'd been too preoccupied taking in the scene to notice my exchange with the medical techs.

"Sky," he said. "What are you doing here?"

I shrugged. Hadn't I wondered that myself?

"Being helpful," I said. "I think."

"Didn't I ask Connors to bring you to the other side of the house?"

"She got away from me, Chief."

That, naturally, was from Officer Connors, who'd shoved past Hibbard and Hornby after following me through the door. All of a sudden the hallway felt really crowded.

It had also gotten increasingly tense in there, due in large part to Vega's obvious unhappiness with Connors and me. He stood frowning at us without comment and then returned his attention to Jerred.

"Okay . . . so Ms. Blodgett finds the body," he said. "Do we know how she got in the door?"

"It was open," Jerred said.

"Open as in slightly ajar? Or wide open? Or just unlocked?"

"Unlocked, sorry," Jerred said. "Ms. Blodgett was bringing in her dog for a dental cleaning. She works at City Hall . . . I think in the county clerk's office or something. Told me she has an early meeting tomorrow morning."

"Actually, she's with the human resources department," I said. "The meeting's at eight a.m. sharp . . . I had to clean the main conference room today to get it ready. Corinne must have arranged to drop off Zsa Zsa tonight, figuring she'd be too rushed tomorrow."

Chief Vega gave me a look. I wasn't sure at first if it was because he appreciated the information or was annoyed at being interrupted. Or because the monkey had clambered up onto my shoulder and started making nervous squeaking sounds. After a second I decided it was a little of all three.

Meanwhile, he'd turned back to Jerred. "Corinne arrives with the dog, lets herself in the door. How come she doesn't go around to the office entrance?"

Jerred shrugged. "Beats me."

"You didn't ask?"

"No, sir." Jerred had gone from shrugging to squirming in a blink. "I, ah, left that to Clarke. Since he's outside taking her statement—"

"Corinne probably used this door because it's already after seven o'clock," I said. Not that anyone had asked me. But I thought I knew the answer to Vega's question, and felt bad watching Jerred cringe.

Vega shot another glance in my direction. "And the reason that's important is . . . ?"

"Dr. Pilsner's office hours are only till five. If she made special arrangements with Corinne, she probably asked her to use the home entrance. That's where she would have expected to be."

"At home as opposed to in the office."

"Right."

Vega tugged his chin. It was another gesture I'd gotten used to seeing when he was deep in thought.

The squeaking monkey aside, everyone in the hallway was quiet as Vega slowly moved around

Dr. Pilsner's crumpled body and studied it from various angles. Though I tried not to look, my eyes staged a mutiny. All at once, the full, harsh reality of Gail's death—and the certain violence with which it had come about—almost bowled me over. Possibly as a defense mechanism, I pictured her alive and rubbing noses with Skiball while giving her a checkup. That's one way cats make friends and express affection.

Ski has a shy temperament and doesn't do her nose-rubbing bit with many people besides me.

"Anybody here notice this entrance is open?" Vega had stepped over to a paneled door to the right of the stairwell.

"Slightly ajar, sir," Jerred clarified with a nod.

He hadn't meant to sound wise. On the contrary, I think he was trying to impress the chief. But I jumped to his rescue anyway.

"The door leads straight into Gail's offices," I said. "I don't think she keeps . . . *kept* it locked."

"What makes you say that?" Vega asked.

"Hardly anyone in town locks the doors in their homes. Also, her reception desk's on the other side. And her file cabinets. I've seen her rush in and out plenty of times without stopping to lock or unlock it."

Vega was looking at me again, not a hint of annoyance in his eyes now.

"Thanks, Sky," he said simply.

I stood there without quite knowing what to say. Have I mentioned that Mike was a crime reporter? Because he was. And it struck me that he'd never once thanked me for helping him with an investigation.

Vega had reached for the handle of the partially open hallway door.

"You wait here," he said to Jerred, flicking a glance past him at the EMTs. "Nothing gets moved till I'm back . . . understood?"

"Yessir."

Vega tapped my arm. It startled the monkey, who leaned over and conked the top of Alex's head. "Did you see that?" he said. "The monkey hit me."

"Sorry," I said timidly. "I think he's a little upset."

Vega looked up at the monkey's face, then down at mine.

"Does that thing really *belong* here?"

I shrugged. Carefully, so as not to tip the monkey off his shoulder perch. "He isn't a thing. He's a monkey. And at the moment we don't know where he belongs."

Vega finally gave out a sigh and waved Connors over.

"You and Sky come with me," he said, pushing the door the rest of the way open. "I want to talk to the kid who's supposed to have done this."

Chapter 3

We've all heard nightmarish stories about how it is to discover your home's been burglarized. A person opens his or her front door, finds everything in the place upended, and realizes someone's violated what's supposed to be a safe harbor. A lot of people will tell you that's the worst part of it—even more upsetting than the destruction and loss of valuables. The deep and unnervingly intimate sense of violation.

I got a hint of that entering Dr. Pilsner's office. The best I can describe the feeling is to say it was like inhaling secondhand smoke . . . except its impact on my mind and emotions was immediate instead of gradual. There was shock, horror, outrage, and a feeling of absolute helplessness that I'd be unable to shake for a long, long time afterward.

The office had been tossed. I saw that instantly as I came through the doorway from the foyer, following Vega into the area behind the reception desk.

Two tall metal file cabinets stood to the left of the entrance, their drawers pulled way out, almost everything that had been inside them scattered around the room. It was the same with the desk drawers. Whatever they'd held had been dumped. Open and half-open manila file folders lay amid their spilled contents. Papers littered the desktop and chairs, covering almost every inch of the floor so you could hardly avoid stepping on them. There were patient records, order forms for veterinary supplies, drug pamphlets . . . all kinds of stuff.

I paused just inside the door, looking at the shambles around me, the monkey agitatedly scooting down from my shoulder and snuggling into my arms again. I felt him tremble as he burrowed his head into my chest.

Vega produced a low whistle. "Somebody really went to work here."

Connors seemed about to comment when I heard an electronic bleep. He unclipped a two-way radio from his belt, identified himself.

"For you, Chief," he said, and then held the radio out to Vega.

Vega stood looking momentarily puzzled, as if he didn't know why the call hadn't come on his own two-way. Then it must've dawned on him that he wasn't in uniform. He sighed, took the radio from Connors, and raised it to his ear.

"Right . . . right," he said. "Okay, got you. Call on my cell if you need to get hold of me again."

He signed off, noticed my curious expression.

"That was Larson," he explained. "Most of the animals have been rounded up. There's a farm out near Wingaersheek Beach that'll take them in till their owners are located. A petting zoo down in Peabody's also offered help if we need it."

The news came as a relief. I hadn't counted the animals I'd seen running loose, but guessed there must have been more than a dozen.

Vega handed the radio back to Connors. After a moment he went around the desk to the waiting area and peered down a corridor to his left. I knew it led to the examining rooms, surgical room, and kennels. A door from the kennel gave directly to an attached barn out back, where Gail had boarded larger animals.

"The kid's in one of those examining rooms back there," Connors said. He motioned down the hall. "Poole and Woodburn are keeping him company."

"You said you caught him running away from here?"

"Right. He was three or four streets down. Headed toward Broadway."

"Any weapons on him?"

"No."

"Drugs?"

"No."

"Nothing at all in his pockets?"

"Just a wallet with a few bucks in it. And a cell phone."

"And you're positive he didn't toss anything?"

Connors shrugged. "What with those animals running loose, we couldn't take more than a quick look . . ."

"Well, now's your chance. I want a thorough neighborhood search. Front yards, hedges, sewer gratings, you name it. Also, has anyone checked out the clinic's medical supply cabinets?"

"Not sure, sir. I know *I* didn't."

"Then get on it. See whether it looks like anything's missing from them. Especially ketamine and xylazine. But also lidocaine, antibiotics . . . whatever other veterinary pharmaceuticals might be kept on the premises."

Connors took a step away.

"One last thing, Ronnie—"

He paused and looked at Vega.

"Talk to the neighbors and see if they heard anything. Between the office being trashed, those animals bolting, and whatever happened to Dr. Pilsner, there must have been quite a racket around here."

Connors gave a brisk, alacritous nod, and this time headed off. A moment later I joined Vega in the reception area.

"You think this was about stealing drugs?" I asked.

"Could be. A bunch of clinics around Boston have been hit lately. You've heard of ketamine?"

"That's a cat tranquilizer, right?"

"A tranquilizer and a hot club drug. What makes it all the rage is that it has psychedelic effects. The others aren't as popular, but there's still a market for them on the street."

I considered that a second. I'd never felt the urge to mess around with drugs, not even as a teenager. In all honesty I can't claim it was a consciously responsible decision. I certainly got into my share of trouble messing around with *guys*, and was no smarter, more grown-up, or problem free than my friends and classmates who were users. For whatever reason, the temptation just wasn't there for me. In fact, I hadn't ever seriously thought of giving Skiball tranks. Well, maybe once, when she escaped from her kitty carrier and jumped onto the gas pedal while I was driving on Route 128. Though I didn't think that counted.

Killing for drugs . . . it was hard to take in. By no means was I naive; I knew it happened far too often, and intellectually understood what could drive people to it. But grasping it on a visceral level was something else.

If I was going to mull that any further, though, it would have to wait. His hand on my elbow, Vega was gently guiding me toward the hallway.

"Hope you're ready to do some translating," he said.

"*Lista, dispuesta, y capaz,*" I replied in Spanish.

Since he didn't ask what that meant, I didn't tell, and instead carried the monkey along in silence.

Orlando and the officers who'd chased him down were in the second of the clinic's three examining rooms. But I suspected "chased" wasn't the right word, or at least had a considerable element of hyperbole to it. Poole and Woodburn had been with the Pigeon Cove police for three decades, making them the longest-tenured cops in the department. They always rode on patrol together, and I'd been told they had married each other's sisters together in the same ceremony. If their spare tires were any indication, they also ate all their meals together . . . and ate and ate and ate.

I doubted they could have done much running à la Starsky and Hutch without succumbing to cardiac arrest. And I wondered how they could have possibly caught Orlando unless they'd nabbed him by surprise. He had the long-limbed, whipcord-thin physique of a sprinter, and it was easy to see he could have outpaced them without breaking a sweat.

We entered the room to find him slouched on a chair near a stainless steel examining table, his head hung down, his hands tightly clasped on his lap.

I won't describe him to you as a Johnny Depp look-alike, even though he was. My editor at the *Anchor* would call that cheating if I did it in my column, and I try to take constructive advice.

Orlando was a handsome kid. About eighteen or nineteen, with sharply angular features and a mop of tousled black hair, he sported a mustache and a short goatee with a soul patch under his lower lip. He had on black jeans, a brown Ecko hoodie with one of those big embroidered rhinos in front, and black-and-white leather Nikes that I figured must have cost what he earned in a full week as Gail's veterinary assistant.

As Vega approached him, I decided to hang back inside the door till I was needed. With Poole and Woodburn already there guarding Orlando, it was an even tighter squeeze than the foyer.

Then a bunch of things happened in a hurry. First the monkey began making a racket—an excited chittering that brought Orlando up straight with a sudden, electrified jolt. As he snapped his head off his chest, he looked across the room at the monkey and broke into a grin. It quickly got bigger and brighter, spreading from ear to ear.

"*¡El mono!* Mickey! *¡Está aquí!*"

It took the monkey about a half second to react. Squirming against me, he puckered his lips and let out a long, high whoop. I initially thought Orlando's exclamation had frightened him, but then realized what ought to have been obvious. There was no way in the world I could conceive of the happiness on the kid's face making anyone or anything afraid.

As if to confirm that thought, the monkey broke free of my arms and sprang to the floor. It streaked around Vega, between Poole's legs, past Woodburn, and then went scrambling up into Orlando's lap.

"Mickey!" Orlando wrapped his arms around it and continued beaming with unmistakable joy. *"¡He buscado todo el mundo para ti! ¡Me había preocupado mucho!"*

Vega glanced over at me, his face a question mark.

"The monkey's named Mickey," I explained.

"I sort of caught that much," he said.

I shrugged, frowning a little. It wasn't as though I'd been asked to pick and choose which parts to translate. "He told the monkey he was looking everywhere for him."

Orlando nodded fiercely. *"Mickey es un mono que está entrenada por Helping Hand."*

"¿Qué es eso? No entiendo."

"Helping Hand?"

"Sí."

"Una organización que ayuda a las personas minusválidas, señora."

"The monkey was trained by a group called Helping Hand," I said to Vega. "They provide assistance to people with disabilities."

"By giving them monkey companions?"

"Now that I think about it, I remember hearing about the program," I said. "There was a story on the news a while back. I—"

"El hombre de la silla de ruedas . . . Señor Doug-

las . . . fue al hospital," the kid broke in excitedly. I couldn't blame him. It must have been a relief to have someone there who spoke his language.

"He says someone named Mr. Douglas had to go to the hospital," I said. "I'm guessing that's who the monkey lives with, since he uses a wheel-chair."

"*Sí,*" the kid said. "He bring Mickey . . . bring to . . . *¿cómo se dice—?*" He broke off in frustration, wrestling with his command of English. Then he gave me a pleading glance. "*Mickey está aquí esta semana. Vive a la clínica cuando el señor hace sus reconocimientos de médico.*"

I nodded that I'd understood him. "Mickey was staying at the clinic this week. Mr. Douglas boards him whenever he goes in for tests."

"He won't be too hard to find if he lives on the Cape," Vega said. "Sky . . . ask Orlando to tell me what happened here."

The kid suddenly held the monkey closer to him. I got the feeling he didn't need that inter-preted. But I asked anyway.

"*¿Qué pasó aquí?*"

He took a deep breath. Then, speaking mostly Spanish, he told me he'd been feeding the animals out in the barn—and waiting in the clinic for Corinne Blodgett to bring her dog in at about six thirty—when he heard loud noises in the office, went to see what caused it, and found three men in there going through the file cabinets. The instant he saw them, he knew they were robbing the place.

"*Uno tenía una pistola,*" he said.

I looked at Vega. "He says one of them had a pistol."

"Can he describe these men for me? Were they white? Black? Latino?"

"*¿Cómo?*"

"*Blancos,*" he said finally. "White."

"All three of them?"

"*Sí. Todos.*"

"And what age were they?"

"They young," Orlando said in broken English. "*Mi edad, como yo. . .* maybe like me."

"And how old would that be? Nineteen? Twenty?"

"*Dieciocho.*"

Vega looked at him. "Eighteen, right?"

"*Sí.*"

Vega was nodding. "Did they say what they were after?"

Orlando didn't wait for me to interpret.

"They want money," he said. "*Y drogas.*"

"Drugs?"

Orlando nodded.

Vega was watching his face. "Tell me how the animals got free."

Orlando didn't answer.

"Do you understand?" Vega said. "The animals—who opened their cages?"

Orlando just sat there with his arms around the monkey. He seemed upset by the question.

"Sky," Vega said, "can you ask him . . . ?"

"I understand, *sí*," Orlando said at last.

Growing more visibly distressed by the second, he explained in rapid Spanish that the robber with the gun turned it on him when he'd run into the waiting area, and then asked him where the money and drugs were kept. He said he didn't tell them—*"No porque era un héroe"*—not because he was a hero but because he was so frightened he'd gotten tongue-tied, especially trying to speak English, and because he had no idea where Dr. Pilsner locked away her cash and her credit receipts. The robbers had thought he was deliberately keeping the information from them, gotten angry, and started releasing the animals, bringing him into the kennels to watch at gunpoint, telling him they wouldn't stop until he told them what they wanted to know.

Vega's face was intent.

"Is he saying all three robbers were letting go of the animals?"

Orlando shook his head, held up two fingers. "*Dos* . . . two."

"And the third man?"

"He hold the gun."

"Held it on you," Vega said.

"*Sí.*" Orlando mimicked a man pointing a gun again.

"And then what? Something must've happened in here to scare the three of them off."

Orlando looked at him blankly, turned to me for help.

"*¿Qué pasó en próximo?*" I said.

Orlando nodded his understanding and stroked the monkey's head.

"Mickey," he said.

Vega raised an eyebrow. "What about Mickey?"

Orlando had continued to face me. "*Creo que* Mickey *les habían asustado* . . ."

He was back to talking at light speed. I did my best to keep up, concentrating, once or twice asking him to repeat himself. I didn't want to miss any part of his story.

The robbers were very scared of the monkey, he said. *Muy, muy asustados.* He'd heard one in particular tell that to their leader, the man with the gun, refusing to go near its cage to set it free. Mickey had been swinging around inside it, rattling its sides in a panic, and that spooked all three men. And then Mickey's frantic jumping around tipped the cage over on its side. The door had opened somehow, and the monkey escaped from the cage, screaming with fright, running all over the place before he scampered out into the barn and . . .

". . . that distracted the man with the gun long enough for Orlando to follow Mickey and make a break for it too," I finished translating.

Vega looked at the kid. "Then what? I'm guessing these men wouldn't just let you take off on them without a chase."

Orlando made a confused face.

"Did the robbers run after you?" Vega clarified.

"*Sí*. They run. No catch me . . . I run more fast."

Silence. Vega did that thoughtful neck-rubbing thing he does. Then I heard what I recognized as the sound of a cell phone set on vibe tone.

Vega reached into his pocket, listened, and thanked the caller for keeping him posted. I supposed it was Larson again.

"Okay," he said to me after putting the phone away. The entire call must have lasted a minute. "Tell Orlando I want to hear the rest."

I told him. But he didn't have much to add. Orlando said he'd managed to shake the three robbers almost right away, although he thought they might have decided to take off before someone noticed all the animals on the street and realized there was trouble at the clinic. Once it seemed they were gone, he went looking for Mickey for a little while, but then realized he'd better call the police. He was rushing toward the station house on Broadway when Poole and Woodburn came driving by with their sirens on, saw him running, and picked him up—

Vega made a stop gesture with his hand.

"Hang on," he said. "Didn't you think to come back here *before* heading over to the station?"

Orlando sat uncomprehendingly, and I put the question to him in Spanish.

He still seemed confused. "*¿Por qué?*"

Vega shot me a glance.

"Did he just ask *why*?" he said.

I nodded, meeting Vega's gaze. Now we were the ones who looked baffled . . . as did the pair of veteran cops in the room with us.

"Ask him if it occurred to him to see if Dr. Pilsner was okay," Vega said.

His eyes went from mine to Orlando's, held on them as I posed the question.

The kid just shrugged.

"No," he said. "Dr. Pilsner *no estaba aquí. Fue a hacer recados.*"

My jaw dropped. He'd answered that Dr. Pilsner wasn't home. That she had gone out to run some errands. Was it possible . . . ?

Orlando was suddenly looking at me.

"*¿Es algo malo,*" he said.

I faced him, thunderstruck. He didn't know. I was sure of it. He didn't know what had happened to Dr. Pilsner.

"*¿Es algo malo?*" he repeated, tensing as he read the shock on my features.

"He's asking if something's wrong with Dr. Pilsner," I said to Vega.

The chief's eyes had zeroed in on the kid. Though his expression wasn't quite disbelieving, I could tell he was miles and miles away from trustful.

"Dr. Pilsner is dead, Orlando," he said flatly. "Do you understand me?"

Orlando stared at him in silence.

"Do you understand?" Vega said.

Orlando sat there gaping at him a second or two. Then a huge shudder ran through him and he clapped his palms over his eyes.

"Orlando . . .," I began, then realized I didn't

have the slightest idea what to say and gently put a hand on his shoulder.

A moment later he let out a small, muffled moan and started sobbing convulsively, still covering his eyes, tears streaming down between his fingers, dripping down over his cheeks and beard until it glistened with wetness.

I kept my hand where it was and exchanged glances with Vega. We both knew I had no need to translate anything more for Orlando, not right then and there.

Clearly, he'd understood.

Chapter 4

"Are you okay, Sky?" Vega said, his hands on the steering wheel.

"Fine," I said. And paused. "Well, so-so, I guess."

Vega glanced over at me. I was in the squishy leather passenger seat of his silver Range Rover, looking quietly out the windshield as he drove me home to the Fog Bell. It was about eight o'clock at night, and the town center's elegant old houses were pretty in the twinkle of our old-fashioned streetlamps, the white clapboard Colonials and redbrick Federals lined up one after another behind blossoming trees and lawns.

"I'm sorry," Vega said. "This was some night out."

"It wasn't your fault."

"Which part do you mean? The animal stampede? Mickey the monkey eating your food? Or your winding up as an interpreter at a murder scene?"

"None of those." I offered him a thin smile. "I was glad to help. And besides, Mickey was sweet."

Vega didn't say anything as he turned onto Main Street. I thought of the monkey and felt sorry for him, remembering his sad, wizened little face when the police put him back in his cage. I knew he would be returned to his companion soon enough, but he'd seemed so unhappy being separated from Orlando.

It was the image of Gail Pilsner at the foot of her stairs that really bothered me, though. That and Orlando getting taken into custody. I couldn't let go of either one.

"I don't think he did it," I said. "The kid, I mean."

Vega drove by the post office, and then the big limestone structure of Carlson Public Library, where several tables already stood out front for the upcoming weekend's spring Book 'n' Bake Sale. I noticed that somebody had dropped a big carton of donated books on one of them, and shook my head. In Pigeon Cove, crimes such as theft and murder were normally the furthest thing from people's minds.

"Orlando hasn't been charged with any crimes," Vega said after a moment.

"But you arrested him."

"We brought him to the station for a formal interview."

"In handcuffs."

Vega nodded slowly. "That's standard procedure," he said. "We're entitled to hold him overnight without pressing charges. If we decide there's no basis, he'll be released."

"And if you decide the opposite?"

"A public defender's on her way up from Salem. The kid'll be treated within his legal rights."

I wasn't sure that answered my question. In fact, I knew it hadn't.

"Do you believe he murdered Dr. Pilsner?" I asked.

Vega hesitated. A few blocks ahead of us, the Fog Bell Inn stood on the corner of Carriage Lane radiating rosy pinkness from foundation to rooftop. Pink building exteriors violated town ordinances that were practically traceable back to the Pilgrims, but my friend Chloe, who owned and ran the B&B, was ordinance-proof. It's hard to explain why. Like all true enchantments, Chloe-magic astounds and mesmerizes without ever baring its secrets.

"I'm going to share some thoughts I probably shouldn't," Vega said at last. He glanced at me and our eyes briefly connected. "Cop business."

I studied his handsome face as he returned his attention to the road. Maybe I've already mentioned this, but in the entire time we'd been exclusive, Mike Ennis had never readily shared his newspaper reporter's business with me. When he did, it was almost always because I'd backed him into a corner.

"Got you," I said, hoping I didn't sound as goopy as I felt inside. "This conversation stays between us."

Vega drove by the Art Association building. "Orlando's story doesn't wash," he said. "There are discrepancies. Things that just don't add up."

"Such as?"

"What he told me about the thieves being after money and drugs. Remember when I had Connors check out the med cabinets?"

I nodded yes.

"Well, they were untouched," Vega said. "Their doors are locked . . . There's no broken glass . . . Nothing appears to be missing."

"And those pharmaceuticals you were concerned about—were they still inside the cabinets?"

"Connors found bottles of ketamine, xylazine, all the rest." Vega shot me another quick look. "They were in plain view on the shelves."

I considered that. "I don't get it. Orlando claimed the robbers threatened to shoot him unless he told them where Gail stocked the drugs."

"And that he was so terrified he choked on the words," Vega said. "The reason they started opening the kennels and pens was supposedly to coerce him into talking."

"But why bother? I mean, they tore the office apart. How could they have missed the drugs if they were in plain sight?"

"They couldn't," Vega said. "Not a chance."

I sat quietly looking out the window. Though nobody would ever confuse Pigeon Cove, Massachusetts, with Rome, Italy, both were built on hills, and as we rolled onto the downside of one its steeper grades, I could see where Main Street ended at the narrow jut of land called Gull Wing, bending out into the harbor with its saltbox shops and fishing wharves.

"Wow," I said after a while. "That totally contradicts Orlando's explanation for how and why the animals got released."

"And why the gang had a gun on him."

"Wow again," I said, shaking my head. "None of this makes sense."

"There's more besides," Vega said. "I figured the commotion in the office must've been pretty loud, and that somebody nearby had to notice it ... You probably heard me ask Connors to knock on neighbors' doors."

I nodded that I had. "Did he turn up anything?"

"Yeah," Vega said. "He's the one who called on my cell while we were talking to Orlando. The woman next door—her name's Heidi Parsons or Paterson; Connors wrote it down—she told him she heard the racket over the sound of her television, and that it startled her. So she turned down the volume to try to find out what was going on."

"And?"

"She heard dogs barking. At least two different men shouting in keyed-up voices. Then a woman's scream and a loud crash. And then the men shouting again."

"Did she say what they were shouting?"

"She didn't know."

"I'm guessing that's because she couldn't make it out clearly enough?"

Vega shook his head. "Didn't know as in 'couldn't understand their language,'" he said. "She insists they were hollering in Spanish."

I squelched the urge to say something as moronic as "Triple wow." Instead, I silently recalled Orlando's claim that the three men who'd broken into the clinic were English-speaking Caucasians.

"Now maybe you get why we took Orlando into custody," Vega said. "I'm not sure how much to believe of what he told us. There's too much wrong with the picture for me to consider anything he says trustworthy."

I wondered whether I agreed.

"You know, I'm good at solving puzzles," I said. "Jigsaws, brainteasers, it doesn't matter what kind. Sit me down by one of those what's-wrong-with-this-picture diner place mats and I'm content."

Vega smiled. "Maybe my real mistake tonight was not taking you out to Chuck E. Cheese."

"There's always next time," I said, smiling back at him. "I really am compulsive about it, though. Guess it's tied to the same mental circuitry as my clean-freakiness. I can't help looking for order when it isn't plain to see. I get very logical and methodical about trying to make things fit together. It's a challenge I can't resist . . ."

"And you're trying to figure out how Orlando's story jives with what happened at the clinic."

I struggled with my answer a moment. "That's the weird part. On the one hand, yes. On the other, I'm having trouble processing it."

"Logically, you mean?"

"You saw how Orlando reacted when he found out about Dr. Pilsner," I said, nodding. "You saw him fall apart, same as I did."

Vega sighed.

"I've seen a lot of guilty people manage to look very innocent," he said. "But I'm not saying you're wrong that he was convincing."

And for that I was grateful.

As we neared the Fog Bell, I was also grateful to see lights on behind the tall, pedimented downstairs windows. It was a good indication that Chloe was home. When she wasn't, her husband, Oscar, would stalk around the house turning off light switches everywhere but in the back parlor, where he relentlessly practiced his clarinet playing. With the tourist season still a month off, and no guests, Chloe had been out and about a lot—gone so much, in fact, that I'd gotten curious about where she was spending her time. If I hadn't known her so well, and she was any less

the social diva, I might have suspected she was
heading out on naughty tête-à-têtes . . . but that
just wasn't Chloe.

Anyway, I wanted to visit with her for a
few minutes before heading up to my apartment.
I'd had a rough night and knew it would help
settle me.

Now Vega eased the Rover to the right,
stopped against the curb near the yew hedge edg-
ing the inn's front garden. Then we sat in the
SUV's darkened cab, the heater blowing softly to
oust the unseasonable chill of the night.

"So," he said, shifting around to face me.
"You're home."

I sat looking at him. "Been some eventful night,
huh?"

"In all the wrong ways," Vega said. "Sky, I've
waited a long time for our date. And I wish it had
turned out differently."

I gave him one of those combination shrugs
and nods. "There'll be others."

He smiled. "I hope . . . that is, I didn't want you
to be disappointed."

His green eyes met my brown ones, held them.
I felt my heart swell up into the vicinity of my
tonsils.

"I won't be," I said, "if you kiss me."

Vega smiled again. Then he slid over toward my side of the cab, and put his arms around me, and obliged, kissing me long and deeply and probingly as my lips parted against his. And I knew then that if the night *had* gone differently, I wouldn't have wanted it to stop there. Not even close to there.

I might mention that it was the first time we kissed like that. The first time we'd kissed at all since we rang in the New Year together in the City Hall bell tower.

I shouldn't have compared him with Mike. It was terrible of me, I knew.

But as I left the Rover and started toward the front porch, gasping for air, I was thinking Chief Alex did it better.

Chapter 5

I'd reached the top of the front porch when I caught a whiff of something unpleasant, to put it very, very mildly. With my stuffed sinuses knocked partly out of commission, it took me a second to identify the nasty smell.

I stood under the porch light, sniffing, my fingers around the doorknob. I didn't want to believe my nose. Did not. That waft did not belong anywhere near Chloe's enchanted palace—it was an abominable juxtaposition. But there was no mistaking its trademark foulness. Only one thing in the world could have made it.

My face crinkling in protest, I entered the parlor. As I'd suspected, Chloe had company. She stood in the kitchen near the dishwasher, her beefy guest seated with his back to me at the breakfast table.

"Sky, dear, you're home from dinner early!" she said, mailing a quick, covert frown over his bald head. "Look who's stopped by to see us just as I was doing the dishes."

Bill Drecksel heaved around to face the doorway.

"Hey-ooh, here's my favorite gal pal!" he said, his walrus mustache flapping over his upper lip like a hairy curtain. "Think spring! I brought ya a special treat to celebrate the season."

I gaped at him numbly. I'd been staying at the Fog Bell going on eighteen months. In all that time, Drecksel had never set foot in the place. And I would have bet his god-awful offering concealed an ulterior motive for the visit.

I heard the dishwasher go into its drying cycle. Meanwhile, Chloe kept stealing pained glances in my direction. Don't ask me how, but even making faces, she managed to project a simple grace in her white straight-leg jeans, a green and white–striped long-sleeve pullover blouse, and a necklace of huge black, green, and brown wooden beads. Though we'd never discussed her age, she looked a well-maintained fifty to my thirty-five. She'd looked a well-maintained fifty when we met a decade before. And I had a hunch she would look a well-maintained fifty when I was a doddering octo-genarian resident of a retirement home.

Although if anything could put years on Chloe, it was the reeking present that had been plunked in the middle of the kitchen table. Stuffy nose or not, it had instantly clawed its way to the back of my throat.

"C'mon while it's hot, Sky." Bill waved me over. "You can't beat my ring bologna quiche, an' I walked this one straight over from my diner after bakin' a fresh batch for the library sale." He grinned proudly and held up a pie cutter. "Even brought along my own servin' utensil."

I looked at him, aghast. Too bad I hadn't known that before, or I might have recommended Chief Alex hand him a cease-and-desist order. But Drecksel's Diner was out on the Wing and we'd driven in from the opposite end of town, which explained why we weren't overcome by the god-awful oven exhaust. The only smell I could imag-ine being in the same offensive league belonged to Drecksel's house-blend coffee . . . and even that noxious brew would be a distant second stinkwise.

"I appreciate the offer, Bill," I said. "Truth is, I'm not too hungry—"

"Hungry, schmungry!" He pulled out a chair to

his immediate right. "Just have a slice. You know I use top-quality Amish bologna, right?"

"I do, Bill . . ."

"Made my once-a-year trip out to Pennsylvania Dutch country for it last week, bought almost forty pounds." He smacked his lips. "Wish I could describe how my car smelled driving back here."

"I can only imagine," I said, trying not to retch. "Anyway, Bill, thanks again. But it'd be a shame to waste good food—I've got a head cold and my taste buds are shot."

He sighed with resignation. "Don't feel you gotta make excuses. I know you gals worry about stupid calories. Trust me, though, some delicacies are worth an exception."

I stood there at a loss for a reply, but leave it to Chloe to come jumping in to my rescue.

"Bill, you're a hundred percent right." She turned the dishwasher off moments into the dry cycle, using one of my efficiency tips. At any other time it would've made me smile. "We do have to watch our waistlines, and I ate less than an hour ago. So instead of picking away at the quiche, I think we'll have two nice, big slices with tomorrow's morning coffee."

Drecksel was visibly disappointed.

"Awright, awright," he said. "You wanna do

that, make sure ya warm it up to get the full flavor. And give yourselves plenty of chunks of bologna."

"I won't forget." Chloe shot another quick look over his head. "Now, if I might ask you something unrelated, Sky . . ."

"Go right ahead," I said thankfully.

"Just as Bill arrived, we heard police sirens at the north end of town—or so it seemed. I know you were up there at Shoko's Minka in the old mill, and I wonder if you noticed anything wrong."

My tongue suddenly became a frozen lump in my mouth. Making it twice and counting that it happened since I walked through the door. Chloe and Gail had been friends. But in my eagerness to change the subject, it hadn't even entered my thick skull that Chloe wouldn't have heard about the murder yet. No way did I intend to announce it while Hey-ooh Drecksel was around to potentially say something stupid and insensitive.

Chloe looked at me, waiting. I stood rooted near the door in my overcoat, anxiously trying to come up with a decent stall.

This time, amazingly, Bill was the one to dangle a bailout.

"You dolls can talk about that siren later," he

said, patting the empty chair beside him. "Look, Sky, I gotta hurry back to the diner and get my other quiches packed for the spring bake sale. But I wanna mention a business proposition to you before I leave."

I sat down without taking off my coat. Whatever Bill was thinking, I had a hunch it was the real reason he'd come bearing his putrid gift. And though I didn't see how any offer he cooked up could possibly interest me, the alternative was to break the terrible news to Chloe in front of him. That was not an option.

Bill had swiveled around in his chair to face me. "Awright, ready?" he said with a huge grin.

I forced myself to nod.

"Tell me if I'm wrong, but you might 'a seen that I finally got some model units for my condo development built."

I was glad my nose was so plugged up, since it kept me from having to hold it. Bill's nicey-nice act stank almost as much as the warm quiche on the table. The Getaway Groves condo park was his dream investment, and after a string of setbacks involving some dirty deeds by our former city council president, its first model units had gone up about a month back.

"Bill, the condos are right behind my office

trailer," I said. "How could I miss them? All I have to do is look out the window."

"Good point. It kinda leads us around backwards to my proposal."

I waited. Bill grinned but didn't say anything else. Besides being annoying, it made me impatient.

"Okay," I said. "What is it?"

"Well, Sky, it's like this." He took a deep breath. "If you can see the condos from *your* window, people in the condos can see the trailer from theirs."

"Uh-huh."

"Thing is, they ain't the same and equal. Catch my drift?"

"No," I said. "Can't say I do."

"Then let me put it to you this way," Bill said. "You, Sky Taylor, lookin' out at a beautiful new half-million-dollar condo ain't the same as somebody inside the condo lookin' out at an old Airstream trailer from when Ike was runnin' for president. In the first case we're talkin' a real pleasure. Somethin' to soothe the eyes, so to speak. In the second case—no offense—we're talking an eye*sore*. And I'm kinda afraid that view might put off would-be condo buyers."

I looked at Bill. Tactlessness I'd expected. And I

wasn't exactly shocked by his ignorance about my restored '62 Tradewind, a classic beauty of a travel trailer if there ever was one—and something I'd been able to afford only after realizing I needed an office for my expanding business, and deciding that taking out a loan to buy it would be my most economical option. But his sheer gall surprised me, considering that the trailer sat on a plot of land I owned outright, having inherited it from our late mutual friend Abe Monahan. And moreover because, as a pure no-strings favor, I'd given Bill a written dispensation to build closer to my property line than town law ordinarily permitted.

I tried not to get too mad at him. It had been a long and difficult night, and I was afraid I might poke him in his big round belly, or maybe dump his disgusting bologna quiche over his stupid, shiny bald head, if I lost my temper.

"Bill, I have no idea what you're hinting at," I said.

"Just that the image I see don't make sense," he said, forming a picture frame in front of my face with his thumbs and forefingers. "A high-class city girl like you sitting in some dumpy trailer . . . uh-uh. It'll never make you happy."

"And I suppose you know what would?"

"Not what. Where." Drecksel grinned at me through his finger frame. "Maybe I never told you, but I own the building my diner's in. Top to bottom. And there's this room right *over* the diner on the second floor that I been usin' for my office." He pulled his fingertips apart, lowered his hands. "Here's the deal, sis. You tow that fossil of a trailer to the junkyard, get it outta sight, I'll let you share the office with me."

"Let me share it."

"Rent free. You just cover all the utility bills."

"It so happens I *like* my trailer—"

"You'll like havin' an office over the diner even better," Bill said. "Listen, I'll sweeten the pot. I know you're into cleaning big-time. Well, you can feel free to clean the joint ta your heart's content. Plus I'll bring you a cup of coffee every mornin'. A bite for lunch too. Speakin' of which . . . you know Stu Redman? The Scottish guy who owns that bookstore?"

"I believe Stu comes from New York," Chloe said. "Isn't that right, Sky?"

"Definitely," I said. Stu affected his Sean Connery accent for reasons unknown. "Brooklyn, in fact."

Bill flapped a dismissive hand.

"Looks like a duck, quacks like a duck," he

said. "Anyway, Stu gave me these bona fide Scottish recipes I'm workin' into my spring menu. Herrings in oatmeal, fer instance. You can have 'em for breakfast instead 'a muffins."

I wanted to gag. "Sounds delectable."

"You bet." Drecksel was grinning again. "And then for lunch there's pigeon casserole."

"Stop."

"You'll love it, Sky. I call my version Pigeon Cove Pigeon Casserole. Get it? You pluck 'n' gut two old pigeons like the ones you can catch on the docks—or like those Beauford sisters from Plum Street, haw! Then you cook 'em in butter with maybe half a pound 'a bacon—"

"*Stop.*"

I was struggling not to blow my cool. Or the contents of my stomach. Though I'm a pretty controlled person, it wasn't easy in either case. Not that Bill noticed, which further annoyed me.

I sat there speechless.

"Awright," he said after a few seconds. "I figured my offer would leave ya overwhelmed, but when it comes to generosity, I don't play beat the buzzer. Why don'tcha sleep on it? Have a slice 'a my quiche for breakfast an' get back to me later on tomorrow?"

I stared at him. There were five or ten responses that would have made a jailbird blush trying to escape my gritted teeth. I reminded my- self that the Cove wasn't the Big Apple, and that Chloe would have preferred I keep it clean.

Fortunately she jumped in before any choice vocabulary could slip out.

"You're right to give Sky overnight," she said. "I'm sure a single bite of your delightful baking will make her decision a cinch."

Bill hawed. "If you didn't know me better, you'd probably figure I brought the quiche as a bribe, huh?"

"Why, Bill, you're reading my mind."

He stretched and pushed himself up from his chair, pie cutter in hand. "Well, gotta hotfoot it outta here—those quiches are waitin' for me."

"Best be on your way, then," Chloe said with a bright smile. "Thank you again for dropping by."

Bill gave an exaggerated wink. "Don't mention it," he said. "I still owe Sky a cup 'a Drecksel's Special Blend from maybe a year ago. You two va-vooms come into the diner together, I got ya both covered, no charge."

And with that, Chloe came around the table and walked him to the door. Still smiling, she fur- tively wiggled her fingers behind her back so I'd stay put. When Bill had left, she returned to the kitchen and sat back down opposite me. Her eyes were serious and the smile had fled her face.

"Now that we're alone, you can tell me what's wrong," she said.

I frowned soberly. "Am I that much of an open book?"

"No," she said. "At least not to Bill, you weren't. Nor to most other people."

"But you aren't most people."

"We've shared too much for you to fool me. I saw your face when I asked about the police sirens. And I knew something serious was on your mind."

I sat looking at Chloe a moment and finally nodded. "It's about as serious as anything gets," I began, and then told her.

Chapter 6

At around ten o'clock I said good night to Chloe and went upstairs to my apartment. Though she'd been stunned to hear about Dr. Pilsner, she took it better than I could have hoped, staying pretty composed as I gave her the distressful news. Maybe, I thought with a weird little twinge, because it was the third murder in town since I'd moved up from New York. The idea Hibbard and Hornby planted in my mind had firmly lodged there—irrational as it was. Could it somehow be my fault the murder rate was rising in the Cove? Was I a Sky full of dark, big-city rain clouds?

I frowned. *Okay, lousy pun.*

It was too early in the tourist season for Chloe to have guests, and the hall was quiet as I strode to my apartment. Well, not totally quiet. But the kind of quiet that seemed to amplify the everyday sort of old-house noises that normally might have slipped my notice. The creak of wooden floorboards underfoot, the groan of rusty plumbing in the walls, the lisp of a breeze through a window sash.

About halfway up the hall, I realized that one familiar sound I didn't hear was Skiball pawing at the inner part of my door. Skiball paws at lots of different things when she's excited, going at the door once my footsteps come close . . . especially when I've been away for any length of time.

Ski also saves a large repertoire of greetings for after I'm actually *through* the door. There's a narrow oak bench to the right of it just inside my apartment—a guy named Moser Valentine made it for me, carving it from a small oak tree in his yard that was downed in a nor'easter—and Ski generally moves her pawing routine over to it when I sit down to take off my shoes. Or if she's in a subdued mood, she'll do a welcome walk with one forepaw stiffly out in front of her and a hind leg stuck straight out in back. The only way to describe that goofy walk is to say it kind of looks like she's swimming without water. She'll take a few steps, rub up against me, and then tip over flat on her side and start purring.

This is all when Skiball's in a mellower groove. In her more typically hyper state, she'll launch into a happy dance that consists of several minutes of skidding around the apartment to the accompaniment of her own shrill screams and warbling yells. It can be funny unless I happen to have a headache or it's that time of month. In which case it makes me want to scream my lungs out like a maniac too.

I guess you could say my little tuxedo's a study in feline extremes.

Since I couldn't hear her through the door as I approached, I suspected she might be tucked into one of my sweaters on her favorite closet shelf. Not even a major explosion would make Ski lift her head when she's having a deep REM catnap in her own version of a Getaway Groves condo.

The point being that it didn't occur to me that anything might be wrong with her as I entered the apartment. In fact, I was thinking about Mose. I'd met him at City Hall while doing my office cleaning and found him an interesting local character. Besides being a member of the town forestry committee, he was an excellent woodworker and amateur meteorologist.

Mose didn't seem to think I was some kind of (ouch again) stormy Sky, I told myself. Mose, who liked speaking in weather metaphors, had in fact once called me a fresh breeze in town. So why let those crabby emergency techs get under my skin? They couldn't even recognize a monkey when they saw one—let alone a *male* monkey sans trousers.

With this in mind, I shrugged out of my coat, hung it on the rack, then sat down on the bench and leaned over to unzip my boots . . . which was when I saw Skiball crouched *under* the bench.

"Ski," I said, surprised. "What're you doing down there?"

She ignored me, staring straight ahead, all hunched up and silent.

Ski, silent? That caught my attention.

I reached a hand down to rub her nose. She didn't respond. That struck me as odd. Ski loved when I rubbed her nose. When I rubbed her nose, she always purred and turned to mush.

Except she wasn't purring and mushy now. She huddled under the bench, acting as if I were invisible.

"Hey," I said, scratching the back of her neck. "You okay?"

Still no reaction.

A little concerned, I started to pick her up onto my lap. But it seemed to make her even tighter and tenser, and I decided to let her be.

I got up off the bench and went into my kitchen. I kept Ski's food and water bowls in the pantry and wanted to see if she'd eaten.

The bowl of kibbles I'd poured for her before leaving the apartment looked untouched. I didn't see any getting around it now—Ski's behavior was more than a little strange. She always had a hearty appetite.

My brow crinkled. No sense getting worried yet, I thought. I would keep a close eye on her, see whether she seemed back to normal by morning. If she didn't, I could start seriously considering a trip to the vet.

And then it hit me. *A trip to the vet.* Only Skiball didn't have a veterinarian in town. Not anymore. I would have to find a new one. It was a sad thought for many reasons. Gail Pilsner had been gone just a few hours and life was already moving on without her.

I frowned. I didn't want to dwell on that before going to bed, not unless I felt like tossing and turning all night. The best thing would be to take a nice, hot shower and then add some cleaning tips to my new Grime Solvers blog. I always found cleaning therapeutic, and thinking about cleaning worked nearly as well. I'd sit down to work on the blog entry till I tuckered out.

A half hour later I was at the little desk in my bedroom, a fluffy white terry-cloth bathrobe wrapped around my midnight blue New York Yankees pajamas. When I turned on my computer and checked my e-mail, I saw that I'd gotten one from Mike. I looked at the time stamp on the e-mail and saw that he'd sent it at midnight his time. If I was right about the time difference, that would have been about six o'clock in the evening my time.

I stared at my computer screen. The e-mail header read, *Missing You Tonight*.

My finger hovered over the mouse button as I did some more silent calculating. I can add and subtract as well as any second grader, math whiz that I am. In Paris, it was now about five o'clock in the morning. Almost wake-up time for Mike. Almost bedtime for me. It underscored that we were a wide world apart. Or at least half a wide world.

Half a world seemed far enough.

Missing You Tonight.

Swallowing hard, I started to open the e-mail, but my finger wouldn't cooperate. I couldn't click the mouse button.

I hadn't missed Mike tonight. I'd thought of him, but I hadn't missed him. About when he'd been writing the e-mail, I'd been getting ready for dinner with Alejandro Vega. Wondering how slinky I ought to dress. Wondering if I might go to bed and wake up in his arms, and knowing there wasn't really much to wonder about. Because whenever I looked into his eyes, I wanted him to make love to me. And whenever we were together, I couldn't stop looking into his eyes.

If our night had gone as I'd planned, it would not have ended with a kiss in his Range Rover. If it had gone as planned, I would have let Alejandro Vega's kisses sweep me off to a world that was ours and ours alone.

Since it was pretty clear from *how* he kissed me that he'd been prepared to risk catching my cold, I thought.

I sat staring at the screen for another second or two, sighed, and closed the e-mail program with Mike's message unread. Once, I'd have felt guilty about not feeling guilty. Maybe I still did, a little. But just a little.

I opened a new document file in my Grime Solvers folder and started typing away:

Rough night tonight. Don't ask how come, because I don't want to think about it right now. My goal is to lull myself into sleepiness, and I'm

*sticking to the subject of cleaning since it relaxes
me. And since I figure that's mostly why we've*

Three and a quarter sentences into my entry, I
suddenly stopped clacking at the keyboard. I'd
heard the sound of a car pulling up outside.

My bedroom window overlooks Carriage Lane,
which runs along the north side of the house to
cross Main Street. Chloe's garage and one of the
Fog Bell's entrances (there are three) face the lane.
My window's almost directly above the entrance.
The car sounded as if it had pulled up right in
front.

I got up, went to the window, pulled back the
edge of the blinds, and peeked out.

A black Lexus idled almost directly below me
on the street, its passenger door facing the curb, the
beams of its headlights lancing out toward the corner. As I watched, its door opened wide and the
interior lamp went on to allow a glimpse of a man
behind the wheel. He wore a dark overcoat and
had a thick head of silvery hair and was reaching
across the front seat for the door handle. I didn't
think I knew him, but it was hard to be sure. Between the darkness outside, the roof of the Lexus
blocking my view, and my being three stories up, it
was hard to get a decent look at his face.

I stood at the window, my curiosity piqued. It was past eleven o'clock. Nothing stirring outside except that car. What had I been thinking before about the late-night quiet in Pigeon Cove? At that hour, it let you hear sounds that didn't seem to fit. Like the Lexus pulling up to the house. And like the side door of the inn suddenly opening now as somebody stepped out onto the porch.

Carefully easing the door shut, the shadowy figure hurried down the porch steps and then crossed the sidewalk to the waiting car.

My eyes widened. Chloe was one person I would've recognized anywhere. From any vantage, day or night. And just an hour earlier, she'd told me Oscar was already fast asleep. That she was going to join him in bed right after I went upstairs.

So much for that. Standing at my window, I watched her pause on the sidewalk for a quick glance back at the inn. Then she climbed into the Lexus, shut her door, and sat back as the car pulled away into the night.

Too stunned to move, I kept staring out the window at the empty street. Oscar Edwards was bald except for a sparse, messy fringe of white hair. I'd never seen him stalk around the house in anything besides a battered old peasant cap, a pair of plain brown work pants, and a goose-down vest on chillier days. On the rare occasions he *left* the house, Oscar wore a red barn coat with corduroy elbow patches and drove a decrepit Chevy station wagon with fake wood paneling on the sides.

I wondered who the Lexus's driver could be. And then wondered where Chloe had gone with him at that late hour. One thing was clear—it wasn't to bed with Oscar.

It was a while before I let go of the blinds and returned to the computer to work on my cleaning tips. I guess I finally went to bed around midnight, feeling tired and ready for some sleep.

Staring up at the darkened ceiling hours later, troubled thoughts swirling through my head, I conceded that I hadn't been nearly ready enough.

SKY TAYLOR'S GRIME SOLVERS BLOG

Mixed Greens

Rough night tonight. Don't ask how come, because I don't want to think about it right now. My goal is to lull myself into sleepiness, and I'm sticking to the subject of cleaning since it relaxes me. And since I figure that's mostly why we've all gathered together in this dirt-free corner of the blogosphere.

Besides, my night wasn't a total shipwreck. Its redeeming moments were bare and fleeting, but we can't ask for everything, and there were a couple. One of them was noticing that my best friend had put one of my new ecofriendly cleaning hints into practice. It gave me the idea for this entry and that's something to hang my apron on.

I'm calling these tips Mixed Greens because I'm combining new environmentally sound cleaning methods with more traditional ones. The bottom line is that my hints *work*, and that means being careful not to ignore practicality and efficiency when substituting the old with the new—a commonsensical approach as we make a conversion to alternative products and techniques.

Incidentally, you can give Bry the Wonder Guy credit for the name and raising my environmental consciousness. He's made me realize that small changes in the ways we clean—and use our cleaning equipment—can make a big difference. Whether it's saving energy (and cutting down on high home fuel and electric bills), helping to ease the impact of toxic chemicals that infiltrate our soil and food, or reducing the amount of waste containers dumped into landfills, I think these will be helpful to you—and everyone around you.

So . . . here are a few greens to toss in with your old tried-and-trues.

1. Using a dishwasher is nearly always more economical than washing by hand. This is for the simple reason that most of us rinse dishes under a running tap, wasting a whole lot of water. A water and energy-efficient machine will pay for itself over time, since conserving water means lower water and sewer bills.

    You can further cut your energy costs by turning off your dishwasher early in the drying cycle. The heat generated once the cycle begins is enough to dry your dishes without electricity. You should consult your manufacturer's operating manual for information on how to stop the drying cycle, but simply opening and closing the door will interrupt it for most modern machines.

2. There isn't an alternative cleaning concoction I like more than this homemade nonabrasive cleaner: Add a small amount of baking soda to some dish-washing liquid (just enough so that when you mix it in with a fork, the liquid takes on the consistency of a rich hair

conditioner). Dab it on the inside of the oven door and then rub with a small, circular motion. You'll quickly see all the old baked-on splatter lift right off. Next, rinse with cold water and towel dry. Your oven door will sparkle and you won't be breathing in the strong toxins associated with most commercial oven cleaners.

Use this same cleaner for tubs, showers, stainless steel sinks, and even pots and pans. It costs pennies to make. Also, it's one less container taking up cabinet space and winding up in your nonrecyclable trash when it's empty. Finally, it might save you a trip to the store, since most of us keep dishwashing liquid and baking soda as household staples.

3. Before you put away the baking soda, toss a half cup down the sink and tub drains. Follow that with one cup white vinegar and flush thoroughly with hot water. Repeat about every two weeks and you'll never have a clogged drain again (well, unless you dump rags and hair down it).

4. To freshen up your sink's food-waste disposal unit, quarter a lemon, drop the sections down the drain, and then hit the switch, flushing as usual. You can do this while implementing the previous tip or anytime in between. It will eliminate most bad smells from the drain without using chemical deodorizers.

5. Want your house to smell clean besides looking it? Simple. Open the window for a half hour every morning when the weather's nice. No plug-in you can buy is as wonderfully invigorating as fresh air—and it's free!

For extradelightful freshness, treat your room to a vase of flowers from the yard. When choosing your bouquet, don't forget that carnations are pretty but have virtually no fragrance. I always suggest adding a few sprigs of freesia, eucalyptus, or lily of the valley if you have them in your garden.

Chapter 7

As I went downstairs to Chloe's at a quarter to eight the next morning, I found the baking smells in the hall a merciful contrast to the horrid stinkiness of Drecksel's bologna quiche.

They also came as an immediate—if all-too-brief—comfort. After a night when I'd felt my world tilt 180 degrees off its axis, the delicious aroma from Chloe's oven helped reorient it toward normalcy and balance. In fact, I felt better just knowing she was back from her mysterious late-night excursion. After lying awake in bed till around two a.m., I'd finally gotten some spotty rest, drifting in and out of sleep for the next few hours.

One of the times I dozed off must have been right around when Chloe got home—either that or she'd been really quiet, because I hadn't heard her come in. Whatever the case, I'd grown mighty uneasy after watching her slip off into the darkness with the silver-haired Lexus driver ... and could no more stop worrying about her all night than wipe the image of Dr. Pilsner's dead body from my mind.

Standing in the hall now, I still didn't know what to make of her nocturnal outing. But at least she was safely home and ready to start the day with our standard routine—coffee klatching over a tray of her homemade breakfast goodies.

I opened her door, poked my head in. "Knock, knock."

"Sky." Chloe turned from over by the kitchen range and yawned. "Hello, dear."

I paused in the entry to the front parlor. Chloe's voice sounded kind of flat to me. And though she obviously had her face on, I felt she looked tired and bleary-eyed.

There you have it, class ... I said my sense of comfort didn't last long, didn't I? Might as well scratch the word "balance" too.

Chloe never looked tired or bleary. Ever. And she usually singsonged her "hello" to me. Good days, bad days, blah days. It always came out as, *"Hel-loooo-oooooo!"*

I went through the parlor to the dining room, doing my best to hide my befuddled scrutiny. Chloe had on a ribbed black V-neck sweater with a flowery cooking apron over it, and a pair of black athletic running pants with a pale pink double stripe up the outside of each leg. A cell phone case hung from a cord around her neck, its floral pattern matching the apron. Coiled toward the top of her head, her light brown hair was twisted into a low ponytail. It had been secured with a tortoiseshell claw clip.

I supposed things were normal in one respect, then. Chloe was so consistent about putting together nice outfits for herself that a part of me always imagined she did it by snapping her fingers like Samantha in the old television show *Bewitched*. No matter how stressed she was, or what sort of craziness was going on around her, she was always nicely dressed.

I joined her in the kitchen, poured our coffees, added some one percent milk to Chloe's cup, and carried them back to the dining room table. Then I pulled up a chair and sat as she arranged some goodies on her tray with an oven-mitted hand and carried it over from the kitchen.

"Yum," I said. "What have we here?"

"A Gloucester blueberry bread." Chloe smiled and set the tray down in front of me.

"Ah-hah." I picked up a slice and tasted it. "Chloe, this is fantastic."

"Thank you, Sky. Dig in. It's a simple, old-fashioned recipe. Pastry flour, two cups of blueberries, a tablespoon of softened butter, a couple of eggs . . . I add a little grated lemon rind to give it some snap."

"*Definitely* very snappy," I said, chewing.

Chloe took the chair opposite me, her smile broadening. As I sat there eating and sipping coffee, I was almost fooled into thinking I'd let my suspicions get the better of me. Maybe I was reading too much into things.

Then Chloe had to go and yawn again, making me focus on the puffiness under her eyes, and blowing any illusions that she was her normal, positive-vibe-radiating self to smithereens.

There wasn't any avoiding it. I had to ask about her mysterious night ride.

"Chloe, I need you to help me understand something," I said. "Last night when I went upstairs—right before I went up, that is—didn't you say you were going straight to bed?"

She nodded in the affirmative. "I was exhausted. It must have been the news about Gail Pilsner."

"So I'm not mistaken. You did go to bed. With Oscar. In your bedroom."

"Of course. Where else would we have slept?" She gave me a funny look. "What's bothering you, Sky?"

A moment passed. And I'd thought I was putting *her* on the spot.

"Sky?" Chloe urged.

"I don't know," I said.

That drew another glance.

"Well, maybe I do know," I said, exhaling. "I wasn't sleepy after I left here. I mean, I was at first. But then I wasn't. Skiball seemed under the weather and it made me a little worried. So I took a shower and decided to get some stuff done on my computer. Catch up with my e-mail, work on my cleaning-tips blog, and so forth." I shrugged. "After a while I heard a car outside and—"

"That must have been me pulling my Beetle out of the garage."

"Huh? What do you mean?"

"I had to drive down to Gloucester."

I looked at her in disbelief. The car I'd seen her get into was no Beetle. Nor had she done any driving from the passenger seat. Whatever her destination might have been, the silver-haired man had taken her there.

"Chloe, it was eleven o'clock. Where in Gloucester were you going?"

"The drugstore. Lane's Pharmacy here in town closes at nine." She cleared her throat and put a slice of blueberry bread on her dish. "It was an emergency. A minor one—don't be concerned. Oscar had a terrible headache and we couldn't find any aspirin in the house."

I still couldn't believe it. My closest friend was lying to my face. It was wildly, irreconcilably out of character for her. Yet there it was.

She was lying. Straight to my face.

I stayed tight-lipped about the things I'd seen from the window. I wasn't sure of my reasons. But I didn't want her to know what I knew.

"You could've knocked on my door for aspirin," I said. "Or Tylenol. Or whatever. If it's a headache pill, I've got it in my medicine cabinet."

Chloe sat quietly a few seconds, lowered her eyes to her dish. "I didn't know. And as you said, it was late."

"So what?" I kept playing along. "Even if the cabinet was empty, I would've been glad to keep you company."

Now Chloe was sort of nudging her blueberry

bread with a finger. "You seemed so exhausted when you got in," she said. "I—I didn't want to disturb you."

"Better I'm disturbed than have you drive down alone at that hour," I said. "Chloe . . . are you sure you aren't keeping anything from me?"

Her eyes suddenly met mine. "Why would I want to do that?"

She poked her bread around some more as we looked at each other across the table.

"I don't know," I said, trying to hide my disappointment. I'd offered her an out, but she wasn't taking it. She didn't intend to come clean. "Just asking, I guess."

Chloe made a shooing gesture and laughed nervously. "It could be we're both too mystery-minded for our own good," she said. "Not that I'm close to being in your league."

"Huh?"

"Don't be modest." She shooed me off again. "You've actually been involved in solving crimes. I'm just another couch potato *Flipped* fanatic."

She was changing the subject. Or trying to change it. And as much as I didn't want to accommodate her, she'd tickled my curiosity.

"What's *Flipped*?" I asked, taking the bait.

"A television series about ordinary women

who flip their lids and commit murder," Chloe said. "On that new cable television channel . . . the Secret Investigation Network."

"Never heard of it," I said with a clueless expression.

"They call it SIN for short," she said. "*Flipped* is the station's newest hit. A typical episode might be about a wife who shoots her husband and his mistress after catching them in bed, then chops them to pieces and feeds them to—"

"Spare me the graphic details, Chloe," I said. "I'd rather not regurgitate my blueberry bread."

She frowned. "Pardon me, dear. I suppose the crimes can be distasteful. Some have fascinating twists, though. Last week's case involved a society dame who plotted to kill her handyman. They'd gotten into a torrid affair several months before. Then the handyman murdered her husband, making his death seem like an accident. The wife was in on his scheme. She planned to wait a respectable period, collect her husband's inheritance, and marry Mr. Fixit. But it turned out that *he* was secretly carrying on with her grown daughter too. When the wife discovered her lover was also her daughter's lover, she decided to take revenge on him. So she paid her beautiful Venezuelan housekeeper to lure him into—"

"I get the general idea." I hesitated. "Chloe . . . you're positive there's nothing else you want to tell me about last night?"

She stared at me kind of blankly.

"Nothing I maybe ought to know?" I asked.

She kept staring at me for another thirty seconds. Then she shook her head in silence.

What could I do? I was ethically opposed to waterboarding. If she didn't want to fess up, I couldn't make her.

Barely hiding my consternation, I finished my blueberry bread and dabbed my lips with my napkin. The longer I sat at the table, the more tempted I'd be to reveal what I saw from my window. And something told me that it wasn't the time to confront Chloe with the truth. Besides, I had a legitimate reason to hustle along.

"Well," I said, "I'm off to start the day."

"In such a hurry?"

"Skiball's been under the weather," I said. "I want to take care of whatever's wrong with her."

The vacancy in Chloe's expression was suddenly replaced with concern. "I hope it isn't too serious."

"Don't think so," I said. "Probably it's just a hair ball. But, well, with Gail Pilsner gone . . . I've got no choice except to check the local phone book for another vet."

Chloe pressed her lips together. "There's Dr. Ruth Lester over on Brook Street."

"Dr. Ruthless?" I said. "You've got to be kidding. People do nothing but gripe about her being a rip-off. And a mean rip-off, at that."

"Unless you want to head down to Gloucester, I'm afraid she's your only nearby option. Gail was so special . . . I don't know what would've happened to our dogs without her."

I looked at her. "What dogs?"

Chloe gazed back across the table for a moment, lifted her coffee cup, and sipped. She seemed a bit disconnected again. "I meant the Cove's dogs. In general. We have so many of them. Even more dogs than cats. Probably more per household than anyplace else in Cape Ann. Didn't you know?"

"Actually, no."

"Well, I'm sure that's true. But I didn't mean to change the subject." She cleared her throat. "The truth is that Gail didn't leave much room for competition."

I considered that. The Gloucester Animal Clinic didn't take patients without a prescheduled appointment. Also, I had back-to-back cleaning jobs in the Cove starting at noon. Even if I could talk Ski's way into the Gloucester clinic on last-minute notice, driving back and forth would take a while . . . and force me to cancel out on my clients.

Still, I really hated to put things off. Cats usually felt pretty sick by the time they showed symptoms. Or so I'd read somewhere.

"I guess Dr. Ruthless it'll be," I said.

Chloe noticed my glum face. "You don't seem thrilled," she said.

"And you just won this morning's understatement award," I said with a sigh. "Chloe, I know this isn't logical, but I feel terrible about bringing Skiball over to Doc Ruthless. It almost seems a betrayal."

She sat there regarding me. No, *scrutinizing* me. Suddenly she seemed her usual astute self. "Of Gail? Or Skiball?"

I didn't have to waste time thinking about an answer.

"Both," I said, rising to carry my dishes into the kitchen.

Chapter 8

Dr. Ruthless's waiting room was packed when we arrived. This was unusual, not because it was early in the morning, but because I'd figured she had too few patients to ever make a crowd. Of course, a lot of them were probably there because they had no decent alternative. I would've bet half the pets in the room had been Gail Pilsner's regulars.

Toting Ski in her kitty carrier, I went over to the reception desk and got a clipboard with a new-patient chart from the doctor's assistant, a frumpy, detached sort of woman named Madge. Then I found a seat, put Skiball's carrier on the floor between my legs, and started filling out the form.

Ski was making a fuss inside the little carrier

and it kept bouncing around like a Mexican jumping bean. She wasn't happy. I wasn't happy. In fact, not a single animal or human being in the place looked happy, and Madge's rotelike personality didn't help.

In fairness, she'd squeezed Ski in for a nine o'clock exam on very short notice. I tried to be appreciative of it rather than get too put off by her uninviting office manner. Bad enough I had misgivings about her allegedly bill-padding boss.

"Ms. Taylor? Have you filled out the patient forms yet?"

I looked up, pen in hand. Madge had come around from her desk.

"Almost," I said. "I'm just about done with my medical history. That is, Skiball's med—"

"Let me have them." She snatched the clipboard from my lap and gestured toward a hallway to one side of her desk. "Go to the third examining room on the left. The doctor will be with you momentarily." She frowned down at the clipboard. "You didn't provide all the necessary information, but this should do."

"Meh," Skiball said through her carrier's mesh window.

I couldn't have put it any better.

The examining room was simple, institutional,

and cold. Closed venetian blinds, white tiles on the floor and walls. Gail's office was wainscoted with rich natural mahogany. There'd been a wall covered with photos of her favorite furry, feathered, and scaly patients. And she'd had light, airy curtains over the windows. I could picture them blowing in the breeze on pleasant days.

I set Skiball's carrier down on the examining table, let her out, and slipped my finger under the collar she always wears on trips to the vet. Then I scratched her chin to dupe her into thinking I was making nice rather than restraining her. Two years of living with a cat had taught me the incomparable value of trickery and deceit in a loving relationship.

Soon Dr. Lester came in. A short, not unattractive woman in her late thirties, she had frosty blue eyes, a long, thin face, and a bob of ear-length black hair with a straight fringe of bangs cut a bit too short . . . or a forehead that was a little too high, depending on how you looked at it.

A clipboard under her arm, she gave Ski a quick once-over, peeking into her ears and lifting her upper gums with her thumb. After that, the doc made a *tsk*ing sound, leaned back against a stainless steel counter, and reviewed the charts, her mouth screwing up with what might have been distaste. I wondered if she was reacting to the incomplete paperwork, but decided she must have already known about it. Madge would have snitched me out in advance.

Another couple of minutes passed. Dr. Lester studied the papers in pucker-lipped silence. It made me antsy. Silence from doctors never seemed a good sign. And silence from doctors with charts in their hands was especially worrisome. I always felt it meant they were deciding whether to operate, or maybe amputate, which of course was a crazy thought on my part. Still, Ski'd never had a major health problem. All I'd written on the forms was her name, sex, approximate age, and vaccination dates. What could be so interesting about the papers?

I decided to offer my two cents. For the sake of perspective.

"I think Skiball's symptoms are pretty mild," I said. "From what I read on the Internet, she might have a hair ball—"

"Ms. Taylor, we should start by addressing your cat's hygiene issues," she broke in.

I blinked. Skiball groomed herself every chance she got. In fact, she was famous (with me) for her cleanliness, and wouldn't even set foot in a dirty litter box. I wanted to cover her ears.

"Are you sure?" I said. "Skiball's impeccable. I—"

Lester glanced up at me. "In this office, I make the diagnosis."

"I wasn't—"

"Good. You can save your questions until I'm ready." She returned her eyes to the clipboard and slipped a pen from the breast pocket of her frock. "Let's see . . . We need to schedule a dental scaling. Possible extractions."

"What?" I said. "You want to pull her teeth?"

"I said it's a possibility. There's plaque. Don't be fooled because it isn't visible. A buildup could lead to gingivitis or even heart disease." She put a check mark on one of the charts. "While Sky Bell is under sedation, we'll get those claws clipped. Do a professional grooming to remove abundant winter fur. It's that time of year."

"My cat's name is Skiball. As in 'skis' and 'ball,'" I said. "Also, someone had her front paws declawed before I owned her. I'm positive I wrote that information on your form—"

"I meant the hind claws, Ms. Taylor. And please don't interrupt." She stared at me. "Once more and I'll have to ask the cat to leave. This is a busy office. There are other patients in the waiting room."

I stood there at a loss. Somehow I'd thought I was the one who'd been interrupted. A half dozen times. Call me impulsive, but suddenly it was all I could do to keep from grabbing Skiball and heading straight out the door. No need for Dr. Lester to steer me in its direction.

Dr. Lester had gone on scrutinizing the papers on her clipboard. "Sky Bell's information has to be updated," she said. "We should take X-rays, do a full blood workup . . . I'll prep her with intravenous fluid."

"You want to hook Sky—I mean *Ski*ball—up to an IV bag?"

"Correct. A little subcutaneous hydration can't hurt as a precaution before we put her out. I'll prescribe several nutritional supplements for bringing her red blood cell count back up afterward. You can refill them with me once a month. The pills are normally meant for medium-to-large dogs, but we sell applicators that can force them down your cat's throat—"

"Stop!"

"Stop what?"

I hesitated. "Look . . . I already explained that Ski doesn't seem all that sick. I'm really thinking the problem could be a bad hair ball. You mentioned this is the season for it. And so does *Cat MD*."

"The Web site?"

"Yes, I—"

"You believe everything you read on the Internet?"

"I didn't say that."

"Yes, you did," she said.

"No, I did not," I said. "What I told you was—"

"That you found the information online."

"Right. But that isn't the same as believing whatever—"

"So you only believe a *percentage* of the nonsense you read on message boards?"

"I—"

"And what percent would that be? Ten? Twenty? Half of them?"

"Dr. Lester, *Cat MD* is sponsored by licensed veterinarians—"

"Or convicted felons claiming to be veterinarians," she said. "You and I aren't buddy icons floating around cyberspace, Ms. Taylor. Nor is the cat. This happens to be a legitimate, real-world veterinary clinic, where a battery of tests will be necessary for me to proceed with your pet's medical care. If you find the expense too high, we can use a cheaper but less effective anesthetic for her dental work. Defer the clipping. And discuss a payment plan. Though I do attach an added fee for that courtesy, and will require two credit card numbers on file as backup."

I was shaking my head. "I'm not worried about the cost. But Ski shouldn't have to be put through those tests. Her records are all at Dr. Pilsner's office."

"If you say so. Unfortunately, I have no access to them. You didn't even provide the cat's exact age."

"Because I don't know it," I said. "I found her . . . or a late friend of mine did. He was taking a walk and saw her in the middle of the road—"

"Which makes her a mongrel feline and former stray with an uncertain history. It doesn't even give me a pedigree to establish any sort of baseline profile."

That did it. I'd heard enough. Any vet who could foist nail clippings, a dental cleaning, vitamins, unnecessary blood samples, and an IV on Skiball before even *looking* at her wasn't for me.

I hefted her from the examining table into the crook of my arm, snatching up her carrier with my free hand.

Dr. Lester looked surprised. "Where are you going?"

"Gloucester," I said. "Or Beverly. Or Boston, even. Wherever there's a veterinarian who won't literally try to bleed my cat dry, then insinuate she's some ragged stumblebum with a shady past."

I could see that took her aback, and couldn't have been gladder. Maybe I *was* a little impulsive. But I'd grown accustomed to Gail Pilsner's kindness. Dr. Lester seemed not to care whether she was performing a dissection or an operation. No, check that. She seemed not to know the difference between them.

I turned and walked out of the examining room before she had a chance to shove me out. Skiball clung to me tightly, her hind claws digging into my jacket sleeve.

"Reeowwww!" she said.

I didn't blame her for sounding insulted. But I could have done without her mauling the sleeve. I swept past the reception desk to the waiting room. Weaving through the mob of pets and pet owners, I pulled up to a table covered with magazines, rested the cat carrier on top of them, and gently got Skiball back inside despite her complaints.

I must have been halfway through the door when I saw Morrie Silverberg, the ophthalmologist, a few paces down the sidewalk, heading toward the clinic with his mini bulldog, Bits.

There are people who dress for the weather, and people who dress for the season. Morrie fell into the second category. Despite the forty-degree temperature and overcast sky, he'd decided to herald in the spring by wearing sunglasses, a short-sleeved white polo shirt, and red plaid Bermuda shorts that coordinated perfectly with Bits's red plaid collar.

I stood watching them, mesmerized. They made quite a dapper sight. Not to mention a peculiar one. I should mention that neither seemed even slightly chilled.

"Sky! Oh, Sky!" Morrie waved a hand in the air like someone flagging down a Manhattan cab. "Glad to see you . . . I didn't realize your cat is Ruth's patient."

She wasn't, of course. But I didn't feel like getting into it. "What's new, Morrie?"

"Something you'll want to hear about . . . it's a fantastic coincidence that I've run into you this morning. Saves me some cell phone minutes!"

I waited curiously as Morrie took off his sunglasses, slipped them into his breast pocket, and replaced them with regular tortoiseshell frames from the same pocket.

"You know Vaughn Pilsner, right?"

"Gail's ex-husband," I said. "Actually, I've just

heard some things about him. They were divorced before I came to town."

"Those two made some couple. Threw a heckuva party too," Morrie said. He sounded wistful. "I don't know what went wrong. It could have been the age difference—he's twenty years older than Gail. But they stayed amicable afterward."

I nodded but didn't comment.

"Vaughn's my best friend going back to high school, a great fellow," Morrie went on. "Of course, Gail was super too. I always hoped they'd work out their differences." A shrug. "We have our hopes, dreams, and everything in between. I should have known a reconciliation wasn't in the cards once he moved away."

"He lives out West these days, right?"

"Los Angeles. He's a retired banker and still does some freelance consulting there," Morrie said. "Vaughn flew in last night. Says he intends to handle the funeral arrangements."

"He's staying in the Cove?"

"At their home. Well, Gail's home. Vaughn kept the deed in his name so he could cover their property taxes without legal complications. I mentioned they stayed on good terms, didn't I?"

I nodded.

"Anyway, Sky, your name came up during our conversation," Morrie said. "I could tell it pained Vaughn tremendously to find Gail's clinic a wreck. Then I remembered you used to tidy it up, and gave him your telephone number . . . I hope you don't mind."

"Not at all," I said. "It was nice of you to mention me."

"He can use your help. Not just with the office, but the entire property. Seeing it go downhill would compound the tragedy, don't you think?"

I hadn't considered it but realized I agreed. "It would be a shame, Morrie. And I appreciate the referral." Skiball's carrier swung hard, almost making me lose my grip on the handle. She was bouncing impatiently inside it again. "I'll expect Vaughn's call—"

"Wait. I have his contact info right here." He pulled his wallet from the side pocket of his shorts, fished out a business card, and slapped it into my hand. "It's got his cell number and everything."

Which I'd kind of expected from a business card.

"Thanks again, Morrie," I said, dropping the card into my shoulder bag. "You're the studliest."

He beamed at me, his cheeks coloring a little— whether from embarrassment or the cold was anybody's guess.

I patted Bits on the head and took a few steps up the street toward my new Versa, but then paused to look back over my shoulder. One favor deserved another.

"Morrie?"

He was outside Dr. Ruthless's door. "Yes?"

"I should've asked . . . Is Bits feeling okay?"

Morrie smiled. "Not to worry; he's fine. Dr. Lester's very diligent with her reminder post- cards. She already sent me a few about his regular manicure."

I stood looking at him. "You sure he needs it?"

"That's what it said . . . Why?"

"It's just that you might consider buying a clip- per instead."

"And trim Bits's claws at home?"

"Right. It'd be less traumatic for him."

"Hmmm . . ."

"If not today, maybe next time."

He scratched under his chin. "I don't know. Dr. Lester's assistant told me Bits also needed a refill on his vitamin tablets—"

"It's only a suggestion to keep in mind, Morrie," I said, and decided to give him something else to contemplate. "You know those prescription eyedrops you sell at your office?"

"Yes . . ."

"According to the consumer Web sites, they've got something major in common with the pet vitamins."

Understanding dawned on Morrie's face. "I can find the same thing over the counter for half the price?"

I pointed a finger at him.

"There you go," I said, and turned toward my parking space.

Chapter 9

"You want me to drive out and see this ex-Pilsner dude?" Bryan Dermond said.

I was in the kitchen of my Airstream trailer watching him reach into a cabinet above the sink. Exhausted from her trip to the vet, Ski was snoozing obliviously in the overhead compartment to his right, on a shelf she'd staked out as her private loft.

"He's Gail's ex-*husband*, not an ex-Pil—" I broke off my sentence. He'd taken some purified sea salt from the cabinet. "You cooking?"

He shook his head. "Gonna mix some salt and warm water in the bathroom."

"Oh. Any special reason?"

He slid shut the cabinet's door and faced me. "Tell me you don't notice anything different."

"About what?"

"My nose," Bryan said. "C'mon. Make like I'm Socrates."

"Huh?"

"We gain wisdom by asking questions. Check out my nose. What do you see?"

"Well, it's in the middle of your face."

"Skyster, I asked what's *different*."

I sighed. Bry and his girlfriend were film buffs, so I figured they'd seen the old Rossellini movie about Socrates. It went to show how DVD rentals could be damaging to young, impressionable viewers.

I counted his nasal piercings. Ah-hah.

"You got a new ring in your left nostril."

"A new stud. Right nostril." Bry tapped it with a fingertip. "You seriously didn't notice?"

I seriously hadn't. No surprise, considering the huge number he had in his nose, ears, and lips— and other places I didn't want to picture. What did kind of amaze me, though, was the realization that I wasn't too awfully grossed out for a change.

"So," he said. "Guess I should head over to the clinic."

I was quiet a second. Since hiring Bry, I'd learned that not all my clients readily accepted his body jewelry, tattoos, and burgundy-streaked

Goth black hair. Bry's appearance was extreme to put it mildly. While trying to be sensitive to his feelings, I also granted that some people needed a little prep work.

"The salt and water for cleaning off the stud?" I stalled.

"Yeah," Bryan said. "And the crud."

I pulled a face.

"Sorry," he said. "What I meant is it helps heal the skin too. But don't worry; I'm sanitary." He cocked a thumb over his shoulder at the bathroom door. "Got my own glass, cotton pads, and disposal bags in there."

"Thanks."

He shrugged. "So what's the verdict? Do I head over to the clinic when I'm done?"

I hesitated a moment. "I think maybe we should both meet Vaughn," I said. "Together."

"How come? I know the joint inside out. Been cleaning the office and kennels for two months on my lonesome."

"I know."

"And you've got, like, three jobs lined up today. Besides our usual at City Hall."

"Two." I glanced at my Felix the Cat clock on the trailer wall. His pointing white-gloved hands told me it was almost eleven a.m. "The first's in about an hour. Second's at three this afternoon, but it's a quickie . . . that little summer bungalow down on Periwinkle Road."

"Somebody renting it already?"

"No," I said. "But Mrs. Filbert likes it dusted and vacuumed once a month starting in the spring. In case any tourists show up to give it a look."

Bry grunted. "I heard those goobers who broke into the clinic did a real number on it. On Doc Pilsner too."

I nodded slowly.

"Really, Skyster, I'll handle this," Bryan said. "You take care of other gigs and split for home. Maybe catch a nap."

"What about City Hall tonight?"

"We can take my wheels . . . I'll pick you up around sevenish."

I expelled a deep breath, looking him straight in the eye. "Bry, listen, I appreciate what you're trying to do. But Vaughn Pilsner's a retired corporate investment broker who still kind of dabbles for the fun of it."

"Square as a cube, huh?"

I nodded. "I doubt he'll be into the piercing experience."

"Or charmed by my ink?"

"To know you is to adore you," I said. "I just think I ought to make the introduction."

A couple of seconds passed. I hoped I hadn't hurt Bry's feelings. If I had, he was good at hiding it.

Finally he shrugged. "I got five minutes to do my dabbing before we leave?"

"Dab to your nose's content. I'll put out some cat food in the meantime. Ski hasn't had much of an appetite lately. If she wakes up hungry, I'll be on my way to being relieved."

Bry glanced into the cabinet where she was curled in a sleeping ball. "You never gave me the four-one-one on her trip to the vet," he said. "How'd it go?"

"Pick your term for the opposite of calm and relaxing," I said, and then gave him an instant recap. "I'm still not sure what's wrong with Skiball. Or that anything *is* wrong with her. She's just kind of . . . I don't know. Logy, I guess. But I'm definitely not turning her over to the mad Dr. Ruthless."

"There an option B?"

"I'll wait till later to see if she's back to her normal irritating self," I said. "Otherwise, I'd better have the clinic in Gloucester squeeze her in for an appointment."

Bry grunted and carried his sea salt to the bathroom sink, closing the door behind him. I poured some kitty kibbles into a bowl, then sat down at my desk to wait. With everything that had gone on over the past couple of days, I decided to check the calendar appointments on my cell phone and make sure there weren't any that had slipped my mind.

I hadn't even gotten the phone out of my bag when its ringtone sounded. That's Coldplay's "Yellow," if you're curious.

"Grime Solvers," I answered. "Sky speaking."

"Hey there, gorgeous! I see you're up and at 'em early today!"

I suppressed a groan. "I guess I am," I said, and swiveled around toward my window. The Getaway Groves model unit was a few hundred yards behind Abe Monahan's old stone wall—the one he'd built around the property before I inherited it. In fact, the unit's second-story terrace faced my trailer and the little unpaved parking area in back. Something told me that if I held a pair of binoculars to my eyes while looking out at the terrace doors, I would see Bill Drecksel right behind them, scrutinizing me through his own binoculars.

"This is your buddy Billy," he said.

"Uh-huh."

"Or your Billy buddy, you want to flip it around," he said. "That's a joke; get it? Billy buddy. Like those kids' toys—"

"I got it," I said. "Bill."

He cleared his throat. "So what's with you today?"

"I'm not sure what you mean—"

"You sound in a lousy mood."

"Actually, it's that you caught me at a busy time."

"Why?"

"Why am I busy?"

"No, why ain't you in a better mood?"

"I just said—"

"'Cause busy, schmizzy, I know you'd feel better if you tasted my quiche last night," he said. "Or Chloe gave you a warm slice for breakfast like she promised."

"I left in a rush," I said truthfully. "She didn't have a chance to put it in the oven." Which *might have* been the truth, not that I'd checked.

Drecksel exhaled at his end, a big, gusty mouthful of air that was loud enough to hurt my ear.

"Don't think I'm pokin' for compliments," he said. "People know what kind of quality to expect when I bake something for 'em."

"Without a doubt."

"So what'd you decide? Gonna ditch your junk-heap trailer?"

I wanted to bite my tongue. His unmitigated gall was beyond belief. "Bill, I really do have to run . . ."

"Go ahead. I don't mean to put the squeeze on you." He blew more wind. "But keep in mind the advantages of sharin' my office space. And that I can't hold the offer open forever."

"Right," I said, about to cut him off. "Talk to you another time—"

"Incidentally, you see any bears this morning?"

My thumb paused over the phone's End button.

"See *what*?"

"Bears," Drecksel said. "Wild ones."

I shook my head.

"No, Bill," I said. "I haven't."

"Not that I ever heard of tame bears. Except maybe in the circus or Vegas. Even then I ain't so sure. There's a difference between *training* and taming ferocious animals. Remember that time with Siegfried and Roy? I know they fooled with tigers—"

"Bill, what's this about?"

"Just that I got reports they been spotted in the woods around here."

"Wild bears."

"Right. A whole herd of 'em. Couldn't say what kind . . . You got any idea if we got grizzlies in this part 'a the country?"

"No, Bill."

"How about black bears? Or maybe brown ones?"

I suddenly had a weird sense of déjà vu. It was almost as if I were talking to Hibbard and Hornby again. Except they were idiots without being hustlers to boot. "I told you. I don't know. But I'm pretty sure bears don't roam in herds."

"I'll remember that next time I'm on *Jeopardy!*" Drecksel sounded indignant. "Look, I wanted to give you a heads-up, is all. Say there's a bear outside the trailer. That could mean trouble, dependin' if it's hungry and spots that little cat of yours in the window of the trailer. Or maybe sees you gettin' in or out of your car . . ."

"Bill, I haven't read a single report about bear sightings. And I write for the local newspaper."

"Who said it was in that rag? We real estate developers got our own insider sources. When there's bears in the neighborhood, lemme tell you, property values go down. So you might wanna cash in before the public gets wind of it. Do yourself a favor 'n' vacate the trailer. I'll scrape together a few bucks for the ground it's sittin' on."

How sweet and considerate. "Aren't you worried they might scare people off from buying units at Getaway Groves?"

"Huh?"

"The bears. What's to prevent them from licking their chops over the residents of your condos?"

Bill chortled. "C'mon, Sky, be real. A wild bear looks one way and sees that pile of rocks Abe called a wall around your trailer. Looks the other way, it sees a seven-foot-high steel gate . . . Getaway Groves bein' a gated community. Which one 'a those two obstacles is it gonna hop lookin' for easy chow? Especially since you got a little cat in the window?"

I weighed several replies. But I was trying to avoid profanities and ruled them out. So I did the next-best thing and finally pressed the button to end the call.

"Bry?" I could hear the sink running in the bathroom. "You almost done?"

"Washing up—I'm zipping!"

Zipping? I shrugged, grabbed my bag, and headed out back to wait in the Versa. When Bry appeared from the trailer, I was sitting with all the windows rolled down to let in some fresh air, blithely unconcerned with big, bad bears.

"How do I look?" he said, opening the passenger door.

"Freshly dabbed," I said. "C'mon, it's getting late."

Bry slid in beside me and we zipped on out to meet Vaughn Pilsner.

SKY TAYLOR'S GRIME SOLVERS BLOG

Tight Spots

When we started furnishing my Airstream, Bry and I knew its spotlessness would be our calling card. We also knew we'd be in and out on jobs constantly and didn't want cleaning it to eat up time and productivity.

Keeping a small place tidy presents its own set of challenges, whether it's a trailer, the motor home you're using for your cross-country vacation, your one-room office, or a shoe-box studio apartment.

It sounds obvious, but the best way to keep a small dwelling or workplace clean is to avoid clutter.

With this ground rule in mind, I've got a few more helpful tips for setting up and cleaning small interior spaces.

1. Be picky with your furnishings. The simpler they are, the easier it is to be orderly and organized. Stick to pieces with nice straight lines. Ornately carved table legs and chairbacks might look great in the family home or multiroom apartment, but where space is limited, they gather dust, take longer to clean, and can make for a dingy atmosphere.

2. Hide things in plain sight. An old-fashioned storage chest is the best place for ... well, just about everything you aren't sure where to stash away. Looking through the chest in my Airstream, you'll see extra blankets, office and sewing supplies, seasonal decorations, lightbulbs, paper towels, bottled water, even CDs and DVDs. A chest of this sort can also provide extra seating or double as a coffee table.

3. Opt for natural-fiber area rugs. They can be removed and laundered, or flipped over and

snapped to rid them of superficial dust and dirt. Furthermore, they don't have that nose-itching synthetic/chemical carpet smell that can permeate small quarters.

4. Use sliding doors wherever possible. They're ideal for kitchen cabinets, closets, dressers—you name it. It's a lot easier to maneuver when you don't have to back up when open-ing a door—or dance around it.

5. Taylorian Cleanliness Logic: Small spaces get dusty faster than large ones because the dust has fewer places to settle. Most dust in our work and living places comes from outside, and we can control the amount that enters with window coverings—so it's important to choose them carefully. Mylar shades are a good first cover because they're smooth and easy to clean. They let in light while keeping out heat and cold. A bamboo or rice-paper shade as a second covering offers further protection from outside elements and offers a soothing ambience.

6. Leave your shoes at the door. Think about it. We always hear about washing our hands

often because they pick up germs—and we should. But who knows what we're tracking in on the bottoms of our shoes? If it was on the street, we should be sure to keep it off our floors and rugs.

———————————

Chapter 10

Twenty minutes later Bryan and I were at the Pilsner home. Just last night, I'd run breathlessly from across the road behind Chief Al, stuffed to the gills with sushi. Now I'd again found myself short of breath going up the steep wooden stairs to the door—but for a very different reason. As I may have mentioned, I'd gotten in great shape at Get Thinner's that winter. The climb wasn't what bothered me.

I supposed what did was just returning to the place so soon. When I'd parked the Versa out front, everything I'd seen inside had flashed through my mind. Gail's body in the entry hall, the ransacked veterinary offices . . . everything. I don't know how to describe the way I felt. Not exactly. I can only repeat that the sheer force of those images knocked the wind right out of me. And add that I was almost gasping for air as I reached the hilltop and rang the bell.

Naturally Vaughn Pilsner answered the door before I could pull myself together.

A tall, rail-thin man with a light natural tan off-set by a mane of white, wavy hair, he smiled at me from the entryway, wearing perfectly pressed jeans and a pale blue oxford shirt that matched the color of his eyes. Pushed behind his ears, that snow-white hair fell at least three inches below his collar and instantly caught my attention. So did the fact that he was barefoot, though I couldn't have explained why . . . and yeah, I know I'm a newspaper columnist, a basic requirement of which is that I be able to express myself with words. But when I'm at a loss, I'm at a loss.

"Sky?" Vaughn said in a quiet voice, offering his hand.

"Not to be confused with Bry," Bryan said from beside me. "That's my name tag. Making us 'Sky and Bry' when we're together."

Vaughn's smile grew larger as he shifted his attention to Bryan. I might have cringed otherwise. But he seemed slightly removed without being aloof, and the result was an air of calmness about him.

"I heard you've done a wonderful job with Gail's kennels," he said. "Come on in. It's chilly out here. We can chat in the sunroom."

So much for Vaughn having a problem with Bry's hard-core bodywork. As he led us through the foyer, in fact, he carried himself with such ease that my cringefulness was almost dispelled.

But when my eyes landed on the still-broken mahogany rail along the staircase . . . well, so much for not cringing.

"I truly apologize."

I looked up at Vaughn.

"For what?" I said.

"You were here the night of the attack. Right after they found Gail."

I shook my head. "It's all right."

"No. No, it isn't." He'd remained soft-spoken. "This is a big house. I should have had enough sense to have you come through one of the side entrances."

I stood looking at him a moment. And though I knew people's eyes shaded darker only in sappy romance novels, it seemed to me they'd done just that.

"I really am okay," I said. "But how'd you know? That I was here, I mean. Did you talk to the police?"

"Several times since I arrived in town. Last night, this morning . . . they didn't tell me, though." He hesitated. "I'll explain. But first let's get out of this hall and sit down where it's warm and bright."

He turned down the hall and we followed. Again there was something about his bearing, a sort of quiet serenity, that was infectious. I knew he'd been an investment banker once upon a time, but honestly couldn't see him in that role. His slender build and striking long white hair—not to mention bare feet—reminded me of those British rock stars my mom used to costume in her flower child days. Give him a cloak with stars and crescent moons on it and he would've looked like a crown prince of mystical Avalon.

What was it I said about sappy romance novels?

The sunroom was spacious and airy, with enormous floor-to-ceiling windows overlooking the garden, a skylight with some hanging plants below it, a small couch to one side, and cane chairs around a polished, modern slate coffee table. On a trivet in the middle of the table was a glass French press filled with a rich dark brew. There was a delicate pearl porcelain coffee set on a lacquered tray beside it.

"This is beautiful," I said, looking around from the entry.

"When Gail and I bought this place, it was a porch with rotted floorboards and railings that wobbled," Vaughn said. "She made it what it is." He stood in apparent reflection for a second, motioned us toward the table, and courteously pulled out our chairs. "We have water boiling in the kitchen if either of you prefer tea. The coffee might be a bit strong . . ."

"Strong coffee *goooood*." Bryan grinned as he dropped into the chair beside me. "I'm ready for a caf fix."

I considered giving one of his lip rings a hard twist. "Coffee's fine with me too," I said.

Vaughn lifted the press and poured.

"I bought this in Europe years before Gail and I were married," he said. "I don't recall her ever taking it out of the cabinet . . . She always preferred appliances with electrical cords and push buttons. It surprised me to find they'd been using it."

I looked at him. I didn't want to snoop around in his personal affairs—no, check that—I didn't want to be so blatant about it that he *noticed*. On the other hand . . .

"I apologize for rambling on," Vaughn said before I could finish my thought. "I'm at complete loose ends, I suppose. It's the suddenness of Gail's death. And the circumstances even more so." He sat opposite us at the table. "I won't take too much of your time. Morrie Silverberg highly recommended your housecleaning services. He mentioned you'd already been helping Gail maintain her kennels . . ."

"Actually, Bry's handled that all along," I said. "Gail engaged our services last winter when I had a leg injury—"

"Got piped in the knee by a drunken fisherman working for a nutjob," Bry said. "She was messing around with some married bigwig at City Hall . . . I mean the nutcase, not Sky—"

"I'm not sure we need to go into details, Bry."

"All the expensive stuff around here, I don't want it to seem like you're a klutz gonna break anything," he said, and faced Vaughn. "What happens is Sky's boyfriend brings a stripper home from Boston one night. Then Sky does a good deed and takes her in as a roommate. Turns out the stripper was also messing with the bigwig, who busted up with her before he hired Sky to clean his offices, where she found—"

I kicked Bry under the table, figuring it wouldn't be as conspicuous or potentially gory as the lip-ring twist. Then I reached for my coffee cup and sipped without looking over at him.

"Mr. Pilsner—"

"Vaughn, please."

"Vaughn, I'd be very glad to work out an arrangement with you." I took a brochure from my shoulder bag and handed it to him. "We have monthly and yearly contracts with varying schedules and rates. Though many clients prefer calling us in as needed . . ."

"Like with my high-powered nine-eleven deal," Bry said.

Vaughn looked at him. Then looked at me.

"Last-minute cleaning service," I translated.

Vaughn nodded. "Ah."

I took another sip of my coffee and waited as he gave the brochure a quick glance.

"I think we should continue with whatever agreement you had with Gail," he said, setting it down on the table. "That seems easiest for now, don't you agree?"

"I would, except that we didn't do any housecleaning for her," I said. "Bry's work was entirely in the offices and pet-boarding kennels. Of course, I'd be happy to give you an estimate—"

I stopped talking midsentence, distracted by something I'd heard—or thought I'd heard— elsewhere in the house. And then there it was again. I was on the verge of recognizing the sound when Bry scrunched his eyebrows and turned to Vaughn.

"Yo," he said, sniffing. "That popcorn?"

"Microwavable," Vaughn said with a faint smile. "My ex-wife wasn't alone in her fondness for push buttons."

I was quiet for a long moment. I could hear and smell the popcorn getting done. My thoughts, meanwhile, returned to some of the things Vaughn had said that had gotten my curiosity up.

We have water boiling. They'd been using it. My ex-wife wasn't alone.

I know, I know. I said I wanted to avoid obvious snoopiness—famous last words. There's only so much avoidance a person can take without reaching critical mass.

"Vaughn," I said, "I thought Gail lived by herself."

He shook his head. "I suppose you might call

the little one a houseguest," he said very slowly. "But . . . her son had been with her for some time."

Good thing I wasn't sipping my coffee when he said that. It would've slopped out of my mouth when it fell open.

"The two you have a—?"

"We don't." His eyes met mine.

"Oh. I didn't realize Gail was married before."

Vaughn kept his eyes on my face but didn't say anything. I was just starting to wonder if I should've minded my own business when he suddenly looked behind me at the sunroom's entrance.

I heard the lip-smacking noise even before my head whipped around in the same direction.

There in the sunroom's entry stood Orlando, Mickey the monkey perched on his shoulder. A micropop bag in one furry paw, Mickey was stuffing huge gobs of puffy yellow kernels into his mouth with the other.

"¡Amiga!" Orlando said, beaming at me.

"Whoooo-hooo-oo," Mickey said, spitting popcorn all over the place as he launched from Orlando's shoulder onto my lap.

Bryan looked at me for a second, scratched his

head. Then he turned his attention to Vaughn. "Do I gotta ask which 'a those two's Doc Pilsner's son?" he said.

———————————

SKY TAYLOR'S GRIME SOLVERS BLOG

Bry The Wonder Guy's High-Powered Cleaning 911

Phone beeps, hell-o. Surprise, yer leading man or lady's on the way over. Be sweet to rock the cradle, but you had a busy week and it's a wreck. Condition red? You bet. Major life-funk time? No way. Why? Cuz ya know the main thing's to stay calm. And the reason yer calm is you read this blog and prepared.

Prepared means you've got a basket. Not a picnic basket, but a big, tall standing wicker basket with a cover or floor pillow on top. Either that or a hamper. No cheapo plastic hamper from the bargain store, but something nice. Tortoiseshell, say. Nice.

Now bust it into the visiting room and gather up yer personal carnage. Newspapers and mags, CDs and DVDs and television clickers, pillows and blankets, socks, slippers, empty tissue boxes, bubble gum, pooch and kitty toys, that arts-and-crafts project ya been diddling around with...

you get the gist. Throw it all in that basket or hamper and close it up.

Break time. Take a breath so ya don't pass out. Awright, take two and maybe swig some water. But that's all ya get; it's time to bring out the vacuum cleaner with max intent. Put on the nozzle attachment and do a quick sweep. Suck the dust off yer chairs and the corners and floor around yer table. Same thing with countertops, the television, and your couch and cushions. The joint should look better already—but ya ain't done yet.

Got flowers in the garden? Cut a few and put 'em on the table. No flowers? No garden? Take some fruit out of the fridge and put it in a pretty bowl. No fruit? No fridge? No pretty bowl? Forget this blog and go to some online poker site or somethin'.

As for the rest of us: We got the visiting room ready and the bathroom's next. Dump those towels and washcloths in the laundry and replace 'em with fresh ones. Swish over mirrors, the sink and faucets, shelves, and—last but never least—the toilet with glass cleaner. The room's gonna sparkle. The room is gonna smell good. If you've got a spare cut flower, stick one in and the room's gonna look good too.

Suggestion: Don't put that fruit on display in here. Wouldn't want yer SO getting any wrong ideas about yer eating habits.

The kitchen run comes last. If ya got a dishwasher, load it up. Or else wash whatever's in the sink, stack it in the drainer nice 'n' neat, and you're cool. If there are edibles in sight, put 'em away pronto. Butter, bread, crackers, sugar, cereal—all that stuff. Then wipe down yer surfaces and shake out yer area rugs.

Now open the freezer. Check it for scones, muffins, rolls, or biscuits—ya might get lucky. Pop whatever ya find in the oven and move to the head of the class. Yer baby doll's in for a treat and the crib'll smell like you got a life.

Awright. The joint's in decent shape, and it's all cuz ya didn't lose yer cool. Boyfriend or girlfriend walks thru the door and ya got piping hot scones and coffee ready. Kiss, kiss. Or whatever.

Cut to later. Much later, I hope. BF or GF's hit the road. Ya survived yer midmess crisis and don't want it ta happen again. How ta avoid?

Prevention's the word. Open that big miracle stash basket and put more stuff into the basket, where it belongs. Don't be a slacker; do it now. And take yer time—it'll go faster than ya think. When the next "thought I'd stop by" moment comes, ya'll know who to thank for that basket bein' empty and ready fer more junk.

CUOL,

Bry

SKY TAYLOR'S GRIME SOLVERS BLOG

Time-Savers Times Ten

I've been rushing around a lot lately—say, for, oh, my whole adult existence. But let's zone in. With my cleaning gigs, column deadlines, trips to the veterinarian (not fun for me or my cat), and trying to squeeze an actual life somewhere in between, one important constant is coming home to a relaxing, peaceful haven. And an essential component of peace and relaxation is cleanliness. Dirt is chaos. Chaos equals stress. Stress is not our friend.

You don't have to be Stephen Hawking to realize that every minute we spend hustling through the outside world gives us less time to tidy up the places we live. That puts a premium on saving time when we're busy. And since most of us are busy all the time, I came up with a quick list of time-*savers* for you. Whew!

1. Load your trash can onto a skateboard and roll it to the curb on collection day. The few

minutes it frees up for sipping your tea or coffee can do wonders for starting the morning on a positive note.

2. Take a cue from flight attendants. You'll never see one make a trip through the aisle without picking up or dropping off something. Make it your policy to never go from room to room empty-handed. Put the water bottle back in the fridge or recycle bin, cups and glasses in the dishwasher, the keys in your purse, hang your jacket... You'll be amazed at the differnce it makes in the long run.

3. Label electric cords with plastic bread tabs. The next time you need an outlet for vacuuming, you won't need a GPS unit to help you figure out which to unplug.

4. Spritz your degreaser cleaner on a cloth and wipe off remote controls, phones, and faxes, and any other push button accessories. It not only eliminates grime, but is a proven vaccine for sticky-button syndrome.

5. Stop weeding between stepping-stones and gravel paths. Instead, sprinkle them with or-

dinary table salt. The weeds won't creep back. I try to go out with the shaker late in the day so the dew will help dissolve the salt.

6. While you're outside, put some Velcro strips around your patio umbrella. There'll be no more spinning that big thing to try to find the closing strap camouflaged somewhere in its folds.

7. Wash your dishes by hand? Here's a quick way to prevent oversoaping. Squirt a little dish soap into a spray bottle and fill with water. Mist items like lasagna pans, cookie sheets, and soup bowls, then let them soak. You won't waste soap, water, or rinsing time.

8. Your pet cat laying claim to a living room chair can lead to hairy situations for you and your guests. Place a pretty cloth napkin over the seat as a cover. The next time you actually free it up from kitty, just pick up the napkin before anybody sits down and toss it in your laundry bag. The cat naps save you from the constant hassle of fixing up a furry chair for human use.

9. Throw pillows looking flat? Toss them in the dryer with a fabric-softener sheet. They'll come out fluffy and fresh-smelling. As an added benefit, the dryer's heat helps eliminate bacteria.

10. Having your kitchen painted but don't want splatters on your large appliances? Cover them with inexpensive Christmas tree bags. I try to buy all I can after the holiday season when stores are practically giving them away. Their uses are endless. In fact, I could blog on that subject alone if I had the time . . . which I don't right now!

———————

Chapter 11

"There you have it, Sky," Vaughn Pilsner said, after speaking for five solid minutes. "The truth."

He drank some of his coffee while Mickey the monkey sat on my lap with his bag of popcorn, pushing three or four kernels into my mouth at a time. I knew it wouldn't agree with me that early in the morning, though it was Snappy Movie Theater brand, my favorite. But I hadn't wanted to refuse it and wound Mickey's feelings. Besides, the popcorn wasn't nearly as hard to digest as Vaughn's story. Or what he'd told of it so far.

Bryan, meanwhile, was mostly paying attention to Mickey, who'd been poking his new nostril stud between dips into the microwave bag.

"What's *his* problem?" Bry said, covering his nose to block Mickey's finger.

My mind was elsewhere. "He's staying here till the disabled gentleman he assists—"

"*Señor* Douglas," Orlando said from the couch across the room.

"—Mr. Douglas, thanks, gets out of the hospital," I said, looking at Vaughn. "Isn't that what you explained?"

He nodded. "Shifting capuchin monkeys between caretakers can lead to behavioral problems. Orlando took a qualification course in Boston. We offered to keep him another couple of days in spite of the tragedy we've suffered, and the organization thought it best to accept."

"That much I get." Bry was shaking his head. "I meant I wanted to know why he keeps playing with my stud, not what he's doing here."

I gave him a vague look.

"It sparkles," I said. "That probably caught his attention."

"You got shiny earrings on . . . How come he doesn't touch *them*?"

I shrugged again, thinking it might've been because the earrings weren't conspicuously shining in the middle of my face. But I kept that to myself. I didn't want to insult Bry, who was really pretty sensitive. Making yet another occupant of the room whose feelings I had to consider.

Orlando was my main concern, though—and the reason I was so preoccupied. Wearing a black hoodie and jeans, a police tracking bracelet visible around his right ankle, he'd greeted me with a long, squeezy hug after Mickey jumped from his shoulder onto my lap, then thanked me about ten different ways in Spanish for helping him out last night.

I didn't think I deserved too much credit. All I'd done was interpret for the kid because I happened to be there. It hadn't kept him from being arrested and charged with murder, and it hadn't gotten him released from behind bars. Vaughn had done that by meeting a bond the court had set at a million dollars.

"Fifteen years . . . It's a long time for a wife to keep so great a secret," he said to me now, lowering his coffee cup to the table. "I hope you can understand my reaction."

"I'm not sure," I said, then dropped my voice so Orlando couldn't hear it. "Tell you the truth, I'm not even sure we ought to be having this conversation right now . . ."

"*Está bien*," Orlando said in Spanish. "*Eres mi buen amiga.*"

I glanced over at him as Mickey fed me more popcorn, thinking it was too bad he hadn't stuffed my big fat mouth with it a second earlier. It was obvious I hadn't turned its volume down nearly enough . . . but maybe that was for the best. The kid *had* helped set me at ease.

"Were you ever married, Sky?" Vaughn said.

"Yes," I said. "Eight years."

"And if I may ask . . . was it you or your husband who first decided the relationship was failing?"

I paused. Deep breath. I'd found ways to keep the lump in my throat from sticking there too long. It came back whenever I spoke the words, though.

"Paul died," I said. "Cancer."

Vaughn looked at me for a moment. "I'm very sorry."

I nodded silently, still working on the lump.

"I was into my forties when I met Gail," Vaughn said. "Love caught me by surprise. I'd been contentedly independent my entire life. But I've never done things in half steps. I knew that if I proposed to Gail—and she accepted—I'd hold nothing of myself back from her."

"And you let one mistake change that?"

Vaughn shook his head. "It wasn't something I *decided*," he said. "I couldn't control what was going on inside me. The sense of betrayal."

"Because she didn't confide she'd had a child out of wedlock before you met her."

"No," Vaughn said. "Because she didn't trust me enough to confide it."

I considered that. "But wasn't this years before you met? You told me she was only eighteen when she became pregnant."

"A foreign exchange student in Mexico, yes," he said. "Orlando's father was also attending the university there. From the Dominican Republic. Their affair wasn't serious." He sipped his coffee again. "The paternal grandparents had limited resources, but were willing to raise the child as their own. They offered a good home and a chance for Gail and the father to continue their studies. Gail's parents on the other hand . . ." He trailed off with a quick glance at Orlando. "They urged her to terminate the situation."

I hesitated. Despite Orlando's reassurances, it was awkward talking that openly in front of him. I didn't think it was that obvious, but he must have noticed from across the room.

"*Señorita* Sky," he said with a gentle smile. "*Mi mamá no se avergüenza de mi. Me amó.*"

I turned to look at him, the lump back in my throat. This time I wasn't thinking about Paul. Orlando had told me that his mother wasn't ashamed of him. That she loved him.

Vaughn was nodding quietly and I realized he'd

understood his Spanish as well as I did. "Gail never regretted her decision to have the baby," he said. "The guilt she felt was over giving him up. Even knowing it was best for everyone involved."

"Is that why she kept all this from you?"

"Her reasons were complicated. My family had some local status, while Gail came from a modest background. She once confessed it intimidated her at the start. That she was afraid I'd consider someone who'd given up a child disreputable."

"And what about later?"

"I think keeping Orlando secret from me weighed on her. I truly believe one source of guilt compounded the other until it became too much for her to bear."

I wasn't sure what to say. Then Mickey fed me some more popcorn and pressed my lips shut, forcing me to chew and providing an excuse for my long silence. Finally I had to swallow or have it turn to paste in my mouth.

"I still don't see why you couldn't work things out with her," I said. "If you loved Gail . . ."

"It goes back to what I told you before. About how I'd steered clear of romantic entanglements my whole life. And how I fully commit to a course once I do choose to take it."

I was as much at a loss as ever. Vaughn must have read that uncertainty on my face.

"I've always been a contained person," he went on. "The idea of bonding every part of myself to a woman was difficult for me. But when I fell in love with Gail, I didn't just break through my defensive shell. I cast away its pieces. Willfully, wholeheartedly discarded them."

I let that sink in awhile. I was no expert in human nature. But the elusive part wasn't understanding Vaughn's independence and wounded pride. It was trying to grasp how he could have loved Gail as much as he insisted and still be unable to forgive her. I felt as if I'd somehow missed something.

"It's probably none of my business, but what made Gail open up to you about her past?"

Vaughn was thoughtful, fixing his eyes on mine. "Two years ago, Orlando's grandfather became ill and died. It left his grandmother in desperate financial straits. She could no longer support him. Meanwhile the father had moved on. A wife, a family . . . I don't know much about him." He gave me a meaningful look. "You understand these situations."

I nodded in the affirmative. Orlando had been

unwanted by his own father. Vaughn couldn't have said it outright without hurting the kid.

"When she realized it was time for him to come to the States, Gail finally told me about her son," he went on. "I won't pretend that I reacted well. Not at first. But I can't stress enough that it wasn't Orlando. It was that she'd never told me about him."

"Did you offer to help bring him over here?"

"Dijo que él pagaría por todo," Orlando said before he could reply. *"Para vivir con ustedes."*

I looked around at him just as Mickey prepared to shove more micropop into my mouth. Though he tried to nudge my chin back in his direction with his other paw, I didn't give in. Chittering dejectedly, he treated himself to the popcorn with loud, emphatic smacks of his lips. Showed *me* what I'd lost out on.

Then, from Bryan, "C'mon, quit it! Skyster, don't monkeys have to take naps or anything? He's got popcorn grease all over me."

His voice was muffled—I guessed because he'd covered his nose to fend off another round of stud pokes. And while I had a hunch Mickey's renewed pestering was partly misplaced revenge over my popcorn snub (he'd ignored Bry for the past few minutes), I was too busy contemplating

Orlando's words to worry about it. He'd said Vaughn had been willing to pay for everything. That he'd invited Orlando to come live with them in the Cove. An important piece of the puzzle was still missing. At least one.

I turned back to Vaughn. "I realize you were hurt. But it sounds like you were dealing with the situation. Trying to help."

"I was," he said. "I loved Gail. We'd tried unsuccessfully to have children of our own. How could I not accept her only son?"

"Then what was the obstacle?"

I'm not sure I could have described exactly what I saw in Vaughn's eyes. But they held a bleakness that the sun pouring through the skylight couldn't touch. "Gail felt she had to make up a great deal to Orlando," he said. "She'd never balanced being a wife and mother. And she didn't think she could do it without taking some time. She called it a 'step back.'"

I didn't understand. "Step back from what . . . ?"

Vaughn hesitated. "Me," he said, his eyes bright with tears now. "After I opened myself up to her . . . after all our years together . . . from me."

I looked at him and suddenly wished I'd kept my big mouth shut. Or let Mickey cram it with so much popcorn I couldn't talk. When Vaughn had mentioned a betrayal of trust, I'd taken him to mean Gail's keeping the existence of her son a secret. That he'd left her because of it. I could not have been more wrong.

Before meeting Gail, Vaughn had thought he'd be unable to completely share himself with anyone. But he'd done it. He'd let both the woman he loved and Orlando into his life. In the end, it was Gail who couldn't allow him into theirs.

Chapter 12

"Can you believe it? We just locked a double gig," Bryan said from the Versa's passenger seat. "And how'd you like how I pitched my nine-one-one bargain plan?"

"You're a brainy lad," I said, driving.

"Hey, don't joke. I blogged on it this morning."

"The nine-one-one service?"

Bry nodded. "Posted some tips with that 'Time-savers Times Ten' piece you wrote."

"Brainy and a go-getter," I said. "This is why I made you my protégé."

"The entries rock when you read 'em together. Wait and see. People are gonna be ringing our phone off the hook with emergency calls. The only question's how we'll handle the volume." He held his upturned palm out to me. "C'mon, gimme skin on us bein' Vaughneroo's official home and kennel cleaners."

I kept my hands on the wheel and gave him a sidewise glance instead. "Not so fast," I said, coasting down the street. "He said it'll be next week at the soonest before the kennel's open for business."

"So you're gonna make a low five wait on a *technicality*? Skyster, where's the happy face? I didn't know better, I'd think you were disappointed."

I shrugged. "Vaughner . . . Vaughn, that is . . . still has to hire someone to help with the animals. Maybe a couple of someones. There's nothing to guarantee he'll find the right personnel in time. Or that people will want to bring their pets back with Dr. Pilsner gone—and Orlando caring for them."

"Jeez." Bryan slapped his forehead. "I didn't think of that."

I turned left toward the Morneau Road law offices of Rooney and Cabot, where Bryan would be cleaning that morning. Afterward, I planned to shoot out to the trailer for a quick health check on Skiball and then drive over to my own job at the Ruth Payne Inn off Main Street.

"I keep picturing Gail at the foot of those

stairs. And it's hard for me to see Orlando being responsible."

Bryan grunted. "The cops sure figure he's their guy. He ain't wearing that police ankle bracelet as a fashion statement."

I thought silently about the information Chief Alex had shared with me in confidence the night of the murder. Like the discrepancies between Orlando's account of English-speaking robbers and the neighbor's statement about men shouting at each other in Spanish. And like the police finding the veterinary drugs that were supposedly a main target of the break-in untouched in their storage cabinet. But even though Orlando's story had problems, I wasn't sure it came close to proving him a killer.

A sigh escaped me. "I guess we'll find out the truth sooner or later."

"Yep." Bry contemplatively twisted a spike of his hair. "Since you mention it, I wonder how come Vaughneroo spilled the beans about Orlando bein' Gail's kid? Why tell you the truth?"

It was a question that had already occurred to me. "It could be he just needed to talk to somebody," I said without much conviction.

"But why *you*?" Bry repeated. "I mean, he's gotta know you work for a Cape Ann paper."

I wasn't sure what that had to do with anything. "Maybe, maybe not."

"Skyster, he's best buds with Morrie the eye doctor. And it was Morrie who told him Gail was your client."

"So?"

"So I cleaned Morrie's offices the whole time your bum leg had you out of commish," Bry said. "Take it from me, that dude loves to blabber."

I couldn't argue with that. On the other hand, Bry's reasoning seemed headed onto shaky ground. "I write a personal-view column. Not gossip."

"But your prime cut's a crime reporter, am I right?"

Prime cut? "If you mean Mike . . . ?"

"Look, I'm only asking, what makes Vaughn-eroo figure this stuff won't wind up front-page news?"

My eyebrows crinkled. It had struck me that Bry might not be too far off base after all. Vaughn hadn't gotten to be a successful financier without plenty of intelligence and foresight. Nobody did. If I were in his position, looking ahead to a possible trial, I'd be considering ways to buff up Orlando's image. How bad would it be to get out word that he was Gail's son? And that might have been spinning things too negatively. Maybe the real question was, how *good* would it be for people to know?

"You might have a point . . . Let me think on it," I said after a bit. "In the meantime have a great day."

I nodded toward Bry's window and saw mild surprise on his face as he realized we'd reached the eighteenth-century redbrick Georgian that housed Markham and Cabot's law firm. He'd been too preoccupied with our visit with Vaughn Pilsner to pay attention to the passing streets.

I pulled over and he got out. Going around to the rear hatch, he loaded his cleaning supplies into one of our folding carts, waved at me, then hauled the cart off toward the old brick building.

It took me fifteen minutes to drive back to the South End so I could look in on Skiball. I noticed she'd jumped down from her loft and eaten almost half her food before snuggling up beside my desktop computer for a snooze. *Appetite's normal*, I thought, mentally checkmarking a box on the positive side of my list of health indicators. As I moved around the trailer, she lifted her head and squeaked at me—another encouraging sign. Though I still would've liked some irksome hyper antics out of her, I knew she typically slept the morning away, and was comfortable heading out on my scheduled rounds.

For the record, I didn't make a single bear sighting while leaving or reentering my Versa. Black, brown, grizzly, or other. But maybe bears were like Ski and took early siestas.

The Ruth Payne B&B was three homes in from the corner of Hawthorne and Main, several blocks north of the Fog Bell. In fact, I had to pass the Fog Bell on the way there—and was just approaching it when I saw the black Lexus heading toward me amid the light traffic in the opposite lane.

If I hadn't instantly known it was the same car I'd spotted from my window last night, what occurred next would have pounded—and I do mean *pounded*—that realization into my reluctant mind.

The distinguished-looking, silver-haired man at the wheel caught my eye first. Barely. As his vehicle slid past mine, I saw Chloe beside him in front. It was abundantly clear from her expression that she'd seen me too . . . and that running into me wasn't anything she wanted or expected.

We'd pulled almost alongside each other when Chloe ducked down in the passenger seat and hastily turned her head away from me. A split second later, she raised a hand to shield the side of her face. But it didn't come up quickly enough to hide her sheer and utter panic.

The Lexus continued down Main Street toward the spot where it curved past the foot of the Gull Wing pier. I kept heading north toward the Ruth Payne. My blood roaring in my ears, I glanced in the rearview mirror and saw the Lexus swing around the bend and past the entrance to the Gull Wing. A second later, I took another look.

It was gone from sight. Had vanished around the bend.

All at once, I was overtaken with the urge to turn around and follow. I could call the B&B and claim something unexpected had cropped up. A cleaning 911; thank you, Bry. I could tell Shirley Witherspoon, the innkeeper, it wouldn't delay me very long. Say, an hour. Or I could reschedule at her convenience. She'd understand. This was only an off-season touch-up. It was too early in the spring for guests.

I was reaching a hand out for my dashboard cell phone clip when I stopped myself. Not so much banishing the urge to trail the Lexus, but somehow managing to hold it at bay.

I watched my fingers return to the steering wheel. Chloe was a grown woman. I had no right to spy on her. Whatever was going on was none of my business. Besides, I absolutely was not about to jump to conclusions.

I drove on, gripping the wheel, clenching it as hard as I could to keep my hand from mutinously going for the phone again.

It was her business, I thought again. Hers. Whatever *it* might be. No premature conclusions for Sky Taylor.

If Chloe was having an affair, it would be totally up to her to let me know about it. I was leaving it alone. Forgetting all about it unless and until she chose otherwise.

Sure thing.

I reached for the cell phone and called Shirley to tell her I'd be late.

Natalie Oswald lived in a small, Colonial saltbox midway down Abbott Lane, a quiet, narrow cul-de-sac that ran straight up to one of Pigeon Cove's many tidal inlets. It was known as a fabulous spot for watching sunsets, and local painters often came there late in the afternoon, parking their cars in a dirt parking area beyond the paved road, then walking through a sparse patch of brush to stand their easels on the pebbled shore and capture the light off the water.

Besides me, Nat might have been Chloe's closest friend in town. Certainly she was one of them. Together they'd founded the La Dee Das, an a cappella vocal ensemble that entertained at everything from wedding parties to charitable events and hospitals, and covered every musical style from

Springsteen to Stravinsky. Chloe was your defini-
tive mezzo-soprano. Nat was a rare contralto. At
first, it was just the two of them at La Dee Das per-
formances, but they'd filled in other voice types as
they went along. Now there were between six and
ten women in the group depending on the season,
since a few of them summered in Florida.

As the Lexus wound through town, I'd stayed
well behind it, dropping back every so often,
keeping as many cars between us as possible. It
took a right off Main onto Newman Road, then a
left onto Tweed Street, and another left onto
Markham. When it eventually swung off Markham into Abbott Lane, I kept going for a couple of
hundred yards before reversing direction.

The Lexus was parked directly in front of Nat's
place when I turned down Abbott several minutes later. Cruising past to the end of the lane, I
pulled my hatchback into the parking area, got
out, and strolled back up toward the saltbox on
the opposite side of the street, using the trees lin-
ing the sidewalk for cover. As I'd driven past the
house, I had noticed a driveway on the side facing
the intersection with Markham and a large, semi-
fenced-in pile of firewood on the side looking out
toward the dead end. Either Nat had a surplus of
logs left over from the winter or she'd gotten an

extra delivery to tide her through our unseasonably cold spring.

The woodpile was over six feet high and covered with a blue tarp. Since I barely scratch five six in heels, it would give me ample room to duck if anyone appeared from the house or anywhere else along the lane.

I scooted through an opening in the fence and moved behind the logs, craning my head around the edge of the stack to see whatever there was to see. The saltbox had one and a half stories. Its sharply pitched roof would give the upper level a very low ceiling, but I'd been in similar houses whose owners used the upstairs for storage space, walk-in closets, or even a spare bedroom. The row of windows overlooking the woodpile had tiny panes that showed them to be centuries old—probably the originals installed when the place was built. They caught my attention right away, since most windows of that vintage had been replaced with modern types around the Cove.

But I wasn't stalking around Nat's property to admire her windows. Not that I'd have time for it. Shortly after I first noticed them, Chloe and her silver-haired friend appeared behind one, standing very close to each other in conversation.

I didn't know why seeing them upstairs together startled me. I didn't know *what* I'd expected to see when I decided to follow them. But it did give me a sort of reflexive shock, and I dropped back behind the stacked logs so they wouldn't spot me.

I might just as well have stayed put. Neither of them seemed interested in the outside view. I barely had time to catch a glimpse of Chloe before she turned slightly from the silver-haired man, moved to the window, and drew its shade.

I looked up at the window. Now what? I preferred not to let my imagination run wild. But my imagination had its own distinct preference and it had started romping freestyle through my head. Still, I could think of better places to imagine things than behind a big pile of firewood, where I was bound to be discovered and embarrassed. I wasn't particularly sure what I'd gain by sticking around there too long besides a worse case of the sniffles than I already had.

I told myself to head back to the Versa and stood where I was anyway. Five minutes ticked by. Ten. Then fifteen. I got a tissue out of my purse and wiped my runny nose. I didn't want to be thinking about what I thought was going on upstairs. I didn't want to believe it of Chloe. And what about Nat? Could she be some kind of enabler? Unfortunately I knew that wouldn't be so unusual. Back when I lived in New York, I'd worked with a married guy who used another coworker's apartment to do *exactly* what I hated to think Chloe and her handsome male friend were doing behind the drawn window shade. The part that didn't seem to fit was Nat staying home while they did it. Wouldn't she have left them alone? I wondered about that.

More time passed. The breeze was picking up and I was really starting to shiver. I told myself again that it was time to go. And I didn't budge.

I'd hung around outside for almost forty-five minutes when Nat's front door opened. I pressed flat against the woodpile and almost stopped breathing as Chloe and the silver-haired man walked out, Nat right behind them. The three of them talked on the doorstep for a little while, looking serious. I wished I could have heard what they were saying, but their voices were very quiet. With the wind seeming to gust in every direction at once, though, I wasn't certain it would have made a difference if they'd been any louder.

Finally Chloe kissed Nat on the cheek and the man gave her a brief parting hug. Then they left the doorstep, got into the Lexus, and drove off. Natalie was back inside the house even before they reached the corner of Markham and turned left toward the town center.

I stood thinking. The wind rustled the treetops and, faintly, carried the sound of the inlet's water slapping against the pebbled shore behind me. I looked at my watch. It was almost noon. I'd promised to be at the Ruth Payne B&B by one o'clock. It was only a fifteen-minute drive, so I still had some time to play with. I knew what I wanted to do but wondered if I should go ahead with it. My decision came fast. If I was going to catch my death of a cold, I might as well make it completely worthwhile.

I took a deep, fortifying breath, walked from the lumber pile to Nat's house, rang her doorbell, and waited. Footsteps behind the door, and then it opened a sliver.

Nat was a slim, pretty woman with short blond hair and stylishly red-framed glasses, wearing jeans and a light, short-sleeved bouclé sweater. She looked at me a second through the partially open door and then came out onto the front step.

"Sky . . . Why, hello," she said. "What brings you out this way?"

"Well," I said, "I was sort of looking for Chloe and thought I might be able to catch her here."

Nat gazed at me through her red rims. I noticed

she'd kept her back to the door and pulled it mostly shut behind her, one hand on its edge.

"I wish I could help. But I haven't seen her."

"Not at all?"

"No," she said. "Sorry."

I tried not to let my expression betray anything. "I'm positive she mentioned coming over for a La Dee Das rehearsal."

Nat was shaking her head. "I'm sure you're mistaken. I honestly couldn't tell you when our next practice will be."

"Hmmm," I said. "You're sure you didn't have any other plans with Chloe?"

"Well, there's our Tuesday ladies-only dinner," Nat said. "Several of us go out together. But that isn't till next week."

I scratched my ear. "Guess I must've gotten confused."

Nat looked at me, her hand still extended behind her to grip the edge of the door.

"Okay, then," she said. "I'd love to chat, but I really am busy right now."

I stood without answering as she pulled the door open a bit wider and started backing through it.

"All those million trillion things to do," she said, slinking the rest of the way inside. "Good luck finding Chloe. And tell her hello for me."

"Yeah," I said. "Thanks."

Nat had almost disappeared inside the house now, leaving only her hand visible around the edge of the door. Then she slipped it inside and the door shut in my face.

I lingered on the doorstep a moment, tempted to ring the bell again. But then I dismissed the idea. Nat wasn't going to volunteer what she knew. I wasn't going to tell her what I knew. The net result was a stalemate, which meant I'd accomplished everything I could there.

All those million trillion things.

Starting with lying through your teeth, I thought, and turned down the lane toward my Versa.

SKY TAYLOR'S GRIME SOLVERS BLOG

Cleaning Q&A

E-mail! I get e-mail! And it's usually full of urgent cleaning questions! Here's the latest batch to arrive . . . along with my answers.

PROBLEM

Everyone knows I adore my houseplants. Each week I devote an entire morning to watering. The problem is that I always miss a plant or two among the many in my home and dance studio, causing brown leaves and dry, caked soil. Making my problem worse, I've noticed that dried-out soil doesn't seem to hold water very well. When I do get around to watering the overlooked plants, water spills through the pot bottoms and gets all over my floor. Help, *s'il vous plait!*

—Finch De La Fontaine, MA

SOLUTION

Finch is one of my regular clients in Pigeon Cove. If she lived in a warm climate, a few ice cubes in her hanging baskets would help keep their soil moist year-round. But in our New England winters that only leads to fern-cicles.

Bry the Wonder Guy found a solution to Finch's problem at the local garden center, purchasing a huge commercial-sized outdoor planter (the type you see adorning well-coiffed office and apartment buildings). We placed the philodendrons and spider plants along its outer rim, and the larger plants toward the center, with a few to one side to give the arrangement depth. The enormity of Finch's new potted jungle was spectacular—and she loves how easily she can primp it.

—Sky

PROBLEM

I have a very small guest room with a futon bed that's becoming a big drag. Friends say it's comfortable to sleep on, but very difficult to pull away from the wall and unfold. As a result I keep it open all the time. I also have trouble vacuuming underneath it because the platform is so low above the floor. Any suggestions?

P.S. Love your Grime Solvers blog—I sneak daily peeks at work!

—Robynn C., GA

SOLUTION

Easy one, Robynn. People fall into the habit of having their futon beds right against the wall, but there's no reason you need to conform. Push it just far enough away to let you fold and unfold the frame without moving it. In that new location, opening it and closing it will be a breeze, as will getting your vacuum's nozzle underneath and behind it.

—Sky

PROBLEM

As you know, Sky, my wife and I are professional caterers. Last week while a large cooking vat of gumbo was simmering on the range, I stepped out on the deck for a break and lit up one of my Cuban stogies. I must have been out there longer than I'd realized, because I looked inside to see the gumbo boiling over onto the stove top. Hurrying back in, I needed somewhere to put the cigar while I removed the vat from the heat (we don't keep ashtrays in our kitchen, where smoking's off-limits). So I hastily set it on our old standing chopping block and tended to the stew.

The gumbo was saved. But when I went to retrieve my cigar, I saw that it had rolled across the chopping block's surface to leave a burn mark three inches long. My wife's furious at me, as the block's been in her family forever. Is there any way to remove the scar from the wood?

—Jim DeFelice, MA

SOLUTION

This e-mail from another Grime Solvers client prompted Bry and me to head out to the DeFelice place for a cleaning 911. Luckily for Jim, those old cutting blocks are natural wood. Since it was only a surface burn, we sanded the visibly scorched part of the surface. When all that was gone, we did a very light sanding of its entire top. Next we rubbed in a layer of mineral oil and suggested that Jim let the oil soak overnight.

That took care of his problem and leads me to a couple of general tips. Since cutting-block wood tends to get dry, it should be periodically oiled to prevent it from developing unsightly splits that can be breeding places for E. coli and other harmful bacteria. And while we're on the subject of old wooden things . . . anyone fortunate enough to have an antique cedar chest might want to gently sand the inside to revive its delicious fragrance. You'll find it well worth the relatively small amount of time and effort involved.

—Sky

PROBLEM

I have burned stew on the bottom of my beautiful enamel pot. I removed as much of it as possible and soaked the pot in a sink full of warm, soapy water, but I still have crusted spots here and there. Any suggestions?

—Ellen Carr, AZ

SOLUTION

You're halfway there, Ellen. To get off those stubborn bits of burn, pour just enough water into the pot to cover the bottom, add about one-third of a cup of salt, and let it soak on your stove-top burner overnight. The next day turn on the burner and bring the mix to a boil. That should do the trick!

—Sky

PROBLEM

I'm reluctant to use commercial cleaner on my black lacquer dining room set for fear of it getting that dull, foggy look. But if I don't clean it, it's going to become dull anyway! Are there any products made specifically for this type of furniture?

—Becky Morris, Albany, NY

SOLUTION

Not sure, Becky. I've been as unsuccessful as you finding anything on supermarket shelves. What works well for me is using ordinary tea. Make a really strong pot, let it cool, and dip a plain cotton cloth into it. Then go over your furniture with the cloth and immediately wipe dry with a second cloth. I've always gotten great, shiny, smudge-free results with this method.

—Sky

Chapter 14

At around nine thirty that night, I was in my apartment at the Fog Bell trying to finish a Grime Solvers blog entry through an antihistamine haze when my cell phone rang. I'd changed my ringtone from Coldplay's "Yellow" to "Lovers in Japan," figuring it was time for something more uptempo yet not wanting a total musical departure.

I looked around for the phone, unable to recall where I'd put it. Then I noticed the music seemed to be coming from Skiball, who was snuggled on my computer stand with her tush against the minitower. But though Chris Martin's voice sort of resembled hers when he sang in a high octave, I knew song lyrics wasn't exactly her forte.

"Sorry, Skiball," I said, lifting her off the phone. "I have to unpark you."

She didn't seem too bothered. Which bothered me. Skiball was *not* a sound sleeper. I'd have expected her to leap off the workstation like a maniac when the phone rang. Instead, she'd sort of plopped from my hands onto the rug and wandered off into the next room. She was still way too lethargic. I needed to find a competent veterinarian and get to the bottom of her odd behavior. In Gloucester, Beverly, wherever. But I couldn't put it off any longer. Though I had a full schedule in the morning, I would ask Bry to cover for me and figure out how to make it up to him later. Ski was going to the vet tomorrow without fail.

Meanwhile, I flipped open the phone and glanced at the incoming-call log. The most recent was from *A. Vega*.

I smiled and one-touch dialed Chief Alex's number. The cure for Skiball's funk was still a mystery, but for me this was just what the doctor ordered. Finding out Orlando was Gail Pilsner's son had been hard enough to absorb. Add whatever strangeness was going on with Chloe, then mix in Natalie's cover-up, and you had a recipe for stress and fatigue. The clogged nose I'd gotten from standing out by Nat's woodpile was just icing on the cake.

"Sky, hello," Chief Alex answered. Presumably

he'd read my name on his caller ID display. "Did you get my message?"

"Actually, no," I said. "I think there's a five- or ten-year delay between somebody leaving one for me and my voice mail alert. In a good decade. The wonder of modern communications."

He chuckled. "I hear you," he said. "Listen, I know it's a little late. If this is a bad time—"

"Not at all," I said. "I was messing around on the computer when you called. Nothing important. I just couldn't find my phone."

"I'm glad you did."

"Hm?"

"Find the phone."

"Oh, gotcha . . ."

"And call me back me right away."

I waited, still smiling.

"So how are you doing?" he said.

"Okay," I said. "Considering it's been one of those days."

"Is something wrong?"

"Guess you could say I'm sort of beat. I've been running around a lot."

"Then it's nothing serious . . ."

"Physically, the worst of it's probably my head cold."

"And otherwise?"

"I've got a few things on my mind," I said. "My cat's been acting weird. Not to mention some people I know."

"How so?"

I inhaled, exhaled. "I can't explain."

"Oh . . ."

"It isn't easy to explain, that is," I said, wanting to change the subject. "Anyway, what's up with you?"

"The usual, I guess. Police business. Mainly I've been busy with the Pilsner case. Preparing evidence reports for the district attorney." Chief Alex paused. "Sky, I really didn't call to talk about work. I was thinking . . ."

"Yes?"

"Tomorrow's my day off," he said. "Those Essex County prosecutors are coming up to meet me for dinner . . . but I wonder if you'd like to get together earlier. Say for breakfast or lunch?"

I frowned at the crummy timing.

"Wish I could," I said. "But I was just thinking I'd better get Skiball examined. I have to find out what's wrong with her. *If* anything's wrong."

"Is your veterinarian here in the Cove?"

"With Gail gone, no," I said sadly. "She'd been taking care of Ski from the day I adopted her."

"I probably should have realized," Vega said.

"I'm sorry ... Sometimes as a cop, you're so homed in on solving a crime, you lose sight of how broadly a loss affects people. It seems everyone in town preferred Gail Pilsner to—"

"Dr. Ruth Lester," I said. "Also known as Dr. Ruthless."

"She's that bad?"

"Indescribably worse."

"Uh-oh." He paused. "So where are you bringing Skiball?"

"Good question," I said. "My idea was to drive to a clinic in Gloucester. They open at eight in the morning, so I figured I'd leave around seven."

"You don't have an appointment?"

"Nope. And they supposedly require it. But I'm keeping my fingers crossed they'll squeeze her in."

"Well, then, how about I ride shotgun?"

I hesitated a few seconds, caught off guard.

"Sky?" Vega said. "You don't mind my inviting myself, do you?"

"No," I said. "Of course not. You're just so sweet to offer ..."

"It isn't a big deal."

"It is to me," I said. "You *sure* you want to ride down there?"

"Absolutely. I want to see you, Sky."

Gulp. "Well, then . . ."

"Tomorrow morning, then? Around a quarter to seven?"

"That sounds perfect," I said. "You're on Deacon Street, right?"

"Right. Can't miss my house. The yard sort of wraps around the side of the place. It's a miniature pine forest."

"I'll look for your door through the trees," I said.

I didn't have to. He was already out front on the sidewalk when I got there, holding a Dunkin' Donuts bag in his hands and wearing a brown leather car coat, a gray V-necked sweater, and tan chinos. I realized it was only the second time I'd seen him out of uniform, and the first time in casual clothes. If push had come to shove, I would've cast my raw-animalistic-hunkiness vote for this latest look, though Smartly Suited Alejandro was a close runner-up.

I unlocked the passenger door and he opened it, holding the paper bag out for me. "I got us some doughnuts and coffee," he said. "Figured we wouldn't have a chance to sit down for breakfast."

"Thanks!" I smiled and set the bag between the Versa's bucket seats. "You can put Ski in back," I said, nodding at the bouncing cat carrier beside me.

"She seems pretty agitated. Why don't I ride with the carrier on my lap?"

"Probably because you'd rather not have your trip be sheer hell . . ."

"That would be impossible." Vega's long look into my eyes destabilized my internal molecules. While I willed them into a semblance of cohesion, he got into the car, set the carrier across his knees, and strapped in.

"Take your pick," he said, reaching into the doughnut bag. "We've got vanilla cream filled, chocolate frosted, and powdered cake."

"Powdered cake," I said. "It's unlawful to drive with gooey fingers."

Vega looked amused. "You get a summons, I can take care of it."

"I'll bet."

He unfolded a paper napkin, spread it out across my lap, and half wrapped my doughnut in a second napkin before handing it to me. Then he set my coffee in the cup holder.

"Are you always this thoughtful or just trying to impress me?" I asked.

"Yes," he said. That smile again.

I got us rolling.

"You know the name of the animal clinic in Gloucester?" Vega asked.

"The Gloucester Animal Clinic."

"Clever."

"You think?" I said with a dry smile. "It's on Yarrow Street. Not far from the harbor. Hopefully I won't have trouble finding it."

"I know a great shortcut," Vega said. "In fact, I'll give it to you once we get a little closer."

I nodded. Cops always knew all the shortcuts.

We turned onto Route 127's southbound lane, enjoying our doughnuts and coffee. Skiball seemed to have settled down—her carrier wasn't even bouncing around on Vega's lap. Maybe his even-keeled personality was imparting a contact calm.

"So how're you feeling today?" he asked after a bit. "You *sound* a whole lot better."

"Definitely," I said. "I soaked in a steaming tub for half an hour before bed last night. Can't beat it for shaking off a cold."

"And the other thing?"

"What do you mean?" I asked, knowing full well what he meant.

"Your people problems."

It was a while before I answered. I wasn't yet convinced that I had any right sticking my nose into whatever might be going on between Chloe and Mr. Black Lexus. If I decided to talk about it, it was Chloe who'd be the first, and maybe the last, to hear what I had to say. But I'd been thinking there was something I did have to discuss with Vega. Something I'd left hanging between us for too long. How could I frown on my friend's stealth behavior if couldn't be aboveboard in my own relationships? What sort of hypocrite would that make me?

"Alex," I said. "I . . ."

He noticed my hesitation. "Is anything wrong?"

"No, no . . ."

"You sure?" He kept looking at me. "I thought maybe I'd been hogging the doughnuts."

I sighed. "I need to talk to you about Mike Ennis. About Mike and me."

Vega sat quietly a few seconds, then gave a small nod. "I'd appreciate it," he said. "I was waiting till you were ready."

"I don't know that I am," I said. "Maybe there are some conversations you can't be ready for."

Vega waited, his eyes aimed straight ahead at the road now.

"I'm not some teenager out for kicks," I said. "I'm a woman in my thirties who was very happily married for a long time. I loved my husband.

We'd planned to have kids, grow old together, the whole shebang. And then life kicked those plans into the dirt. The way it does, you know?"

He nodded.

"Mike and I started seeing each other a few months after I moved to Pigeon Cove," I said. "Talk about not being ready . . . I think it was too soon after I'd lost my husband. He wanted an exclusive commitment and I couldn't give it. From that point on, things changed. We went on as if they hadn't for a little while, but nothing felt the same. And finally we couldn't pretend anymore."

"Does that have anything to do with why he took that assignment in Paris?"

I shrugged, my hands on the steering wheel.

"You know the story he's covering, right?"

"Be difficult not to," Vega said. "It was on everyone's lips around here for a while. A beautiful Danvers woman marries some French millionaire, moves to Europe with him, and becomes a murder suspect when her husband disappears six months later. Her name's Damiana Something-orother."

"Wilkes," I said. "At least that's her maiden name. Mike's been good friends with her since they were kids."

"No kidding."

"They even dated in high school," I said with a nod. "Anyway, Mike was a crime reporter for a newspaper in Washington DC before he came to the *Anchor*. The same publisher owns a big, prestigious magazine that offered him a bundle of money for an investigative piece on the case. Mike's friendship with Damiana obviously had a lot to do with it."

"How'd his publisher know?"

"About the personal connection?"

Vega nodded.

"Mike wasn't clear about that," I said.

"He didn't tell you?"

"It isn't so odd. Not for Mike. He's always been cagey about his work. And we weren't sharing a whole lot of things at the time."

"Sounds to me like you have an idea, though."

"My guess is he pitched the idea to the magazine," I said. "He would probably claim taking the assignment had everything to do with a career opportunity and nothing to do with our relationship."

"And you believe he needed some distance."

I shrugged again. "It isn't his fault. If anything, the blame's on my shoulders . . ."

Vega turned to me.

"Were you up-front with him all along?"

"Yes . . ."

"Then you shouldn't feel that way," he said. "I don't think anyone's to blame. None of us knows how we'll handle certain situations till we face them."

I drove on past the Cape Pond reservoir in thoughtful silence. In full foliage the roadside trees largely screened the pond from view, but with the season still young you could see its reflective blue surface through their budding branches.

Vega didn't seem to notice. He'd turned to look straight out his windshield.

"One thing you haven't told me," he said, "is that it's over between you and Mike."

"No," I said. "I haven't."

"Because you don't know?"

"Because I don't." I swallowed. "What I do know is how I feel when I'm with you. When you kiss me."

"But not where I fit in?"

"That has to be your choice. I can't make it about what I want." I glanced over at him. He was still staring out at the road. "Yesterday someone told me he'd spent most of his life being, quote unquote, contentedly independent. That isn't me. I'm not trying to keep my heart locked up in a strongbox. But I do need time."

He turned to face me. "If it was your choice, Sky. About us. What would it be?"

"Truthfully?"

He nodded.

I hesitated again. My cheeks suddenly felt warm. "I would tell you to kiss me the way you did the other night. Only when we're alone somewhere and don't have to be anywhere else for a long time. When you don't have to stop."

I felt his liquid dark eyes hold on me for a while before they turned back toward the road ahead. Good thing they did, too. It might have been dangerous if I'd gone and sunk into them while driving.

It must have been between ten minutes and ten centuries later when I realized we were coming up on Rogers Street parallel to Gloucester's Inner Harbor. At around the same moment, Vega shifted around in his seat to look at me.

"I have to tell you something," he said finally, breaking his silence. "It may not be what you want to hear, but it's important that you know."

I looked over at him, nodding, my heart stroking in my ears. *His choice.*

"I got distracted and missed our shortcut," he said with a smile.

And then I was smiling too.

Chapter 15

"I would suggest leaving the cat with us for observation," said the veterinary intern. A young, olive-complected man named Joralemon, he spoke with a faint Indo-European accent.

I steadied Skiball on the examining table, holding her with both hands so she wouldn't go wildly diving off. Although none of the Gloucester clinic's full-fledged vets would see us without the requisite appointment, I supposed I should have been appreciative we'd been assigned the intern. But Joralemon had barely given her a look in the minute or so since he'd blown into the room, and it seemed to me he should have done that before anything else.

"When you say leave her, how long do you mean?"

"Three nights." Joralemon said. "Three nights minimum, yes?"

I exchanged glances with Vega, who was standing right beside me. Then I looked back across the table at the intern. "Don't you think she ought to have a thorough exam first? I mean, she isn't acting that sick."

"I have recommended a course of action. The cat should be monitored," the intern said. "Our receptionist will give you a list of our rates. But an average stay is fifteen hundred dollars."

"Did you say *one thousand five hundred* dollars?"

"Average, yes?" Joralemon nodded. "Basic charges include boarding, food, and water. Further expenses may arise if medication is administered. I would also order daily subcutaneous hydration."

I was beginning to wonder if he'd studied under Dr. Ruthless. Or if maybe she'd authored some unholy veterinary textbook. "Is she *de*hydrated?"

"No. But a fluid drip is a standard precaution."

"Against what?"

Joralemon gave a frown. "Against many adverse health conditions, yes?" he said.

I stared at him. It hadn't taken long for those questioning yeses to become an incredibly bothersome verbal tic. "Is there any alternative to leaving her for that long? I'm just not sure about it . . ."

"We can discuss a payment plan if cost is an issue, yes?"

More shades of Dr. Ruthless. "That isn't the main reason that I'm reluctant about this . . ."

"I understand."

"No, I don't really think you do," I said. "I'm prepared to leave Skiball if I have to. But before I put her through that sort of trauma, I want to be sure it's needed. She hasn't been away from familiar surroundings since I've owned her."

Joralemon looked irritated. "The cat should be observed. You may wish to discuss expenses with your husband, yes? Then we can proceed with—"

"Sky's a friend, not my wife," Vega said. "And I think she just told you that expenses aren't her foremost concern."

"I hear quite well, yes?" A sigh. "But she must be honest."

I lowered. "Are you saying I'm *not*?"

"Each pet owner must decide if treatment is affordable," Joralemon said. "Otherwise we can find an alternative option."

"What option? What are you talking about?"

He produced another sigh of exasperation. "If one finds veterinary health care exceeds one's budgetary limits, one must have the courage to admit it. Our receptionist can recommend a list of shelters that can place the animal with another owner. If no medical reason is found for euthanization, yes?"

I held Skiball protectively in my hands, my jaw almost dropping. Had Gail Pilsner been the only sane, compassionate, unrepulsive vet in the world?

"You're a lunatic," I said.

"Excuse me?"

"Completely out of your mind." I gripped Ski more tightly as she hunkered on the table, my fingers pressing into her sides. "A bonkers ghoul, *yes*?"

"Sky," Vega said. "Maybe we should just leave—"

"And what? Keep hopping from one veterinary office to another?" I said. "This is becoming a nightmare, Alex. I can't go on with it. And neither can Ski. I have to find out if anything's wrong with her without Dr. Death here putting her in intensive care before she even gets a simple checkup."

He thought a moment. "Hang on to her. I'll go out and talk to the receptionist. Maybe we can see one of the certified vets right here at this clinic—"

Skiball suddenly hiccuped. It had a wheezy kind of sound that made me apprehensive at once.

"Hey, Ski, you okay?" I said. Another hiccup. "Ski?"

She retched. Did it again. Then did it even more violently a third time.

I realized how hard I'd been squeezing her since we'd entered the room, and abruptly eased up on my grip, hoping I hadn't brought about whatever was going on with her. But it didn't stop the spasms. She was gagging now, her mouth wide open.

"*Ski!*" I stared at her with huge, panicky eyes, on the verge of screaming at the top of my lungs.

That was when she when she coughed the hair ball up onto the examining table. A black, yucky, and supremely enormous hair ball about the shape and thickness of my middle finger.

A moment later she settled down, licked her paw, and started grooming herself.

I snapped a look at Vega.

"Well," I said, smiling. "Looks like our problem's solved."

"Yeah." He grinned. "It does."

I scooped Skiball off the table and she cuddled against my shoulder, purring, scissoring my neck between her front paws. Across the table, Joralemon poked her gross special delivery with a pair of tweezers and lifted it up to his eyes for inspection. Then he pulled a tissue from a box on a stand, folded it around the hair ball, stepped on the pedal of his wastebasket, and disposed of it.

"We may wish to forgo observation and send the animal home," he said to me. "The receptionist will bill you for this consultation, yes?"

I was thinking of some choice words for him when Vega's cell phone bleeped. He reached into his leather coat, flipped it open, listened intently.

"Where?" he said into the phone then. His face had grown taut. "You know who found . . . ? Okay, listen, have the men wait right there."

"What's wrong?" I said, staring at him. "Alex . . . ?"

He took hold of my elbow and led me aside.

"We have to head back to the Cove," he said in an urgent whisper. "There's been another forced entry." His eyes were on mine. "It's just like the last one, Sky."

It took a moment before the meaning of that last sentence hit me.

"Oh my God," I said. "Where?"

"Abbott Lane," Vega said. "A woman named Natalie Oswald was found dead in her home."

Chapter 16

As I braked at the police barrier closing off Abbott Lane, I saw Officer Connors in front of it, his patrol car nearby in the middle of the road. His baby-faced partner, Jerred, stood leaning against the parked cruiser with his arms crossed.

I lowered my window. There was an EMS vehicle pulled into Natalie Oswald's driveway up the street, its rear panel doors wide open. Hibbard and Hornby were loading a gurney through the doors, an outline of a human body bulging the white sheet on top of it.

Connors approached the Versa, gave me a brief, curious glance through the window, and then looked over at the passenger side.

"That you, Chief?" he said, a hand over his

eyes like a visor. "Sun's so bright this morning I can hardly see."

Vega leaned across my seat. "The coroner here yet?"

"And gone," Connors said. "Maji sent his new assistant again. Liz Delman. She likes to be in and out, not that this one was too complicated."

"What are you hearing?"

Connors nodded slightly at me in the guarded way police do when talking around civilians.

"Go ahead," Vega said. "It's all right."

"The Oswald woman was shot," Connors said. "Twice in the chest."

I felt my heart thumping and tried to look relatively composed.

"Better let us through," Vega said.

The cops moved aside the wooden barricade and I drove slowly up the lane. Two more cruisers were parked on the street, one behind the other. Several town policemen stood outside the saltbox handling a knot of stunned-looking neighbors. A couple of older women were in their house robes and slippers.

I eased to the curb behind the patrol cars. "Okay if I stop here?" I asked Vega.

"Yes, thanks." He glanced over at me, Skiball's cat carrier on his lap. "You all right?"

I nodded, wondering if I should have mentioned I'd been to that same street—and the very house where the crime occurred—just the day before. But that would have meant telling him what had brought me there, and I wasn't doing it unless I thought it could possibly help with something. Which I didn't. Although it was a definite goose bump inducer . . . and not the only one.

"Has it struck you that things end more or less the same way every time we get together?" I asked.

"I noticed," Vega said. "We'll have to change that."

"Hope it's soon."

"I promise it will be." He paused. "You don't have to wait, Sky. I'll give you a call later on."

"I'd rather not leave."

"I have no idea how long it'll take," he said, looking at me. "Whenever I'm through here, I'll need to head over to the station. File a report, oversee the processing of evidence . . ."

"I can drive you. It's on my way back to the Fog Bell anyway."

Vega looked at me some more. "This isn't a pleasant place to be. I wouldn't figure you'd want to stick around."

I simultaneously shrugged and shook my head. "I knew Natalie," I said. "Guess I'm a little shaky for driving right now."

Which was true as far as it went. It just wasn't the whole truth. I also wanted to quiet any thoughts—unfounded, no doubt—that the coincidence of Chloe and her male friend having been at Nat's house yesterday wasn't altogether coincidental.

"Okay, I'll be back," Vega said. He passed me the cat carrier. "Better keep an eye on the little pest."

I gave a wan smile as Vega reached for his door handle, then watched him walk toward the saltbox and stop briefly to speak with the EMTs in the driveway before he entered. After that, I sat tight for a few minutes, puzzling over what could have happened to Nat. But I wasn't about to learn anything sitting in the Versa, and after a while got tired of it.

Finally I got out and went up the street, bringing Ski along in her carrier. I didn't intend to ignore Vega and go too near the house with her. At the same time, I saw no reason to wait where I'd been. Maybe the bystanders gathered on the street out front could tell me something.

"Well, look who's here."

"Funny we no sooner see the police chief than she appears like magic."

"Yeah, how about that?"

I stopped on the sidewalk and turned toward the emergency techs' voices, thinking I'd been upset enough without having to deal with their deliberately loud, butter-knife-sharp repartee.

"Tell me you two have nothing to do besides bug me at a horrible time like this," I said.

"Tell *us* how it is you show up right when we're on another morgue run," Hornby said.

"Poof," Hibbard said. "Every time. Like magic, I'm serious."

"Only goes to show."

I stared at them. They'd slammed shut their vehicle's rear doors and were looking back at me from the foot of the driveway.

"Show what?" I said.

"We'll give you a hint," Hibbard said. "Four for four."

"That's if you start counting with the Monahan murder."

"If you start with Monahan, right. Otherwise, fair play, we'll call it three for three."

"Not that anybody's calling you a jinx. Which was *your* unscientific expression, you may remember."

I took a couple of steps forward, shaking my head in disgust and disbelief. I knew all about men and women in their profession keeping an emotional remove. But were they really that un-flustered after having wheeled a dead woman into their wagon?

"See you," Hibbard said. "We were just leaving for the morgue anyway."

"Not that she couldn't have thought to say good-bye to us."

"Not that she couldn't have," Hibbard said. "Or hi for that matter."

Hornby harrumphed. "Bet she thinks to say hi *and* good-bye to Chief Kissy-poo."

I froze again.

"What?"

"What 'what'?" Hornby winked at his partner. "We just explained 'what' about something else."

"How many *'whats'* you want us to spell out for you?" Hibbard returned Hornby's wink. "We won't mention this last one concerns a private conversation you were listening in on."

I glared at the techs, ready to shower them with the very same blue spew Joralemon the vet-erinary intern had managed to escape earlier that morning—and I mean language I hadn't used since my days of dodging kamikaze New York cabbies. Before a syllable of that undiluted foulness left my mouth, though, Skiball produced a loud and very prolonged *reeehiiiieeeii* from inside the carrier.

Hibbard suddenly dropped his gaze onto it, trying to peer through the front mesh. "Speaking of 'whats,'" he said, "what's in there?"

"It isn't that wallaby again, is it?" Hornby said.

"I read in the paper it was a chimp or something, after all," Hibbard said. "Not that it makes us less curious about why you lug it around everywhere. And how you get away with bringing it along to possibly contaminate a forensic collection area, though we do have our suspicions."

"Kissy, kissy, poo," Hornby said, trading another wink with his partner just as Skiball made some more noise. This time it sounded kind of like *wow-wow-wee*, a good sign she was back to her usual self.

"Look," I said. "Is there any special reason you two enjoy harassing me?"

"What do you mean 'harass'?" Hornby said.

"There's no reason we'd want to harass you," Hibbard said.

"Or anybody else for that matter," Hornby said.

"In fact, we're being conscientious," Hibbard said. "Trying to warn you that whatever kind of living creature happens to be in there—"

"It actually sounds like an exotic feline, now that I think of it . . .," Hornby said.

"Marsupial, simian, feline, *whatever*, doesn't make a difference," Hibbard resumed, frowning at his partner's interruption. "My point is that it's bound to cause a mix-up. When you consider there's already rumored to be canine involvement in the shooting."

I looked at him. "What do you mean?"

"A dog, for example."

"Possibly a dog."

"You can't exclude other types of canines."

"Though, the incident having taken place in someone's home, you'd assume a dog would be high on the list of candidates."

"Being they're the most common domestic canines," Hibbard said. "Not that you heard any of this from us."

I sighed. "Okay, thanks for nothing. I should have figured you two were playing games."

Their mouths turned down in nearly identical frowns.

"Now we're insulted," Hibbard said.

"And wounded," Hornby said.

"Besides being disappointed, since we were giving you an honest tip," Hibbard said.

I hesitated. Call me a sucker for punishment, but their pained expressions seemed genuine.

"Listen, no offense, but I know the definition of canine," I said, deciding to rephrase my question. "What I asked was how a dog was involved in Natalie Oswald getting shot to death."

The techs looked at each other a moment. Then Hibbard made a lip-zipping gesture and turned back to me.

"Sorry," he said. "We don't want to get in trouble."

"I lose my job on account I talked out of school, the wife won't want to hear any excuses."

"My fiancée neither," Hibbard said, nodding. "Believe me on that."

"If it's got fur, leave it behind, is the rule of thumb," Hornby said. "Take that advice and leave it right there. So you don't blow any homicide investigations when those sleazy defense lawyers come flocking around to pick apart the evidence. Or do I have to say the name Barry Scheck more than once?"

I scratched behind my ear. I wasn't sure whether running into those two had left me more confused or aggravated—and frankly didn't care.

"See you another time," I said, and walked on.

I reached the group of bystanders, stopping at its periphery to seek out any familiar faces. After a quick scan I got lucky. Kimi Fosette from the tourist center was talking to one of the bathrobed older ladies. Or having to listen to her blab her ear off, from the looks of it. When we made eye contact, Kimi's glance practically implored me to rescue her.

I waved and called her name over the buzz of the crowd.

"Excuse me, Amelia," she said to the frantic gabber, pushing toward me. "Sky, what are you doing here?"

"It's kind of a long story," I said.

She nodded her head back at the woman I'd extricated her from, dropped her voice. "Not that your arrival wasn't a godsend."

I gave a thin smile of acknowledgment. "I didn't know you live on Abbott, Kimi."

"I don't," she said. "I'm on Hamlin. The next street over. My yard backs on poor Natalie's." She shook her head. "If it weren't for Nat, I'd never have black-eyed Susans. She starts them in her nursery every spring."

I noticed that her face was very pale. "Kimi . . . do you know what happened?"

"As much as anyone," she said. "Because of what I heard."

"The gunshots?"

"And the rest," Kimi said. "The police took my statement. There was the singing ... and then everything else. It was so sudden. I'd always told Nat to keep her door locked. But she never paid attention. As if nothing bad ever happens in the Cove."

She broke off, shook her head some more. I was thinking about the first part of what she'd told me. "Was Natalie in a La Dee Das rehearsal?"

"No," she said. "She was practicing solo this morning. Her voice was so lovely. She had her studio windows open upstairs, and I was out in the garden to do some early watering. The weather may feel like winter, but our plants can't be neglected. Or everything about spring will be spoiled ..."

Her head sank and she began to cry, the tears spilling down her cheeks.

I put down Ski's carrier for a minute, got a pack of tissues out of my shoulder bag, held it out. "Here. You can keep these."

Kimi nodded appreciatively, pulled a tissue from the pack. "Please excuse me," she said, wiping her eyes and face. "Anyway it was so sudden. What caught my attention was the dog. It sounded excited. And then Natalie stopped singing."

I blinked, recalling what the EMTs had said.

"You heard a dog in Nat's house?"

"Yes."

"A barking dog?"

"No," she said. "Not barking. I suppose you'd call it yelping. Like a puppy. But the sound was clearly coming from Natalie's windows," she said. "The most bewildering thing is that she didn't own a dog."

"You're sure?"

"Oh yes, positive. She was devastated after her beagle, Molly, passed away last year. Natalie talked about adopting when she was ready for another pet. I have a friend up in Maine that runs a rescue center for Norfolk terriers, and we'd planned to go up there together this summer."

I let that sink in a minute. "Kimi . . . what happened after you heard those yelps?"

"It's just as I told the police officer. I heard Nat shout something. And then heard another voice answer her. A man's. I don't think he was speaking English . . ."

I waited. She dabbed her eyes some more.

"Do you know what language it was?"

"I'm not certain," Kimi said. "My guess is that it was Spanish. His tone was very harsh. Very angry. The shots came so quickly afterward—"

That was when I heard Chris Martin tunefully advising lovers to keep on the road they're on. I was tempted to completely ignore the ringtone, but it occurred to me it might be Vega calling from inside the house.

"I'd better see who this is," I said.

Kimi nodded. I think she almost welcomed taking a break from her account of the crime.

A glance at the phone's outer display told me it wasn't Vega after all, but Bry calling from the cell I'd gotten him on our company plan. I flipped it open, held it up to my ear.

"Dudette," he said. "Glad I didn't get your vee-em."

"Bry, listen," I said. "I need to call you back. I'll explain later—"

"We gotta talk right now, Skyster. Like this second. I'm at the Pilsner joint."

I hesitated. He sounded agitated.

"Is everything okay over there?" I said.

"With me, yeah," he said. "But ask about the Orlando kid and his monkey, and I got all kinds of bad news."

Chapter 17

"Have the police contacted you?" I asked.

I was in the living room of the Pilsner home with Vaughn Pilsner, Bryan, and a cat carrier that contained an increasingly stir-crazy Skiball. Before speeding off from Abbott Lane, I'd called Vega on his cell and explained that Bry needed my urgent help. I could tell Vega assumed it involved a cleaning job. In fact, I'd counted on him making that assumption.

"I returned from my morning stroll only minutes before you arrived," Vaughn said. "And I haven't even checked the phone messages."

"And there were none on your cell?

He shook his head. "Mine only works half the time. I'm a bit prehistoric when it comes to using those things."

That didn't quite answer my question, but I left it alone. Thanks to Bry, I knew he'd at least told the truth about walking through the door just ahead of me. In fact, we both were still wearing our overcoats.

Still, I wondered if telling someone a partial truth was the same thing as lying. If the answer was yes, I'd lied to Vega. It wouldn't be long before he found out, though. And that made me feel beyond awful.

I looked at Bry. "Okay," I said. "You'd better let us know exactly what happened."

He shrugged nervously.

"Ain't much besides that Orlando lit outta here, Skyster," he said. "I was in the office cleaning the kennels."

"And he was in this part of the house?"

Bry nodded. "Must've been right here downstairs. The phone rang, an' he picks up. Starts talking real loud."

"Could you make out what he was saying?"

"Nope," Bry said.

"How about whether he was speaking English or Spanish?"

"Dunno. By the time I start paying attention, he's off the phone. But I know right off he's amped about something."

"How could you tell?"

"Like I said, he made a racket. Slams the phone, starts running through the house."

"And then?"

"Then I hear the back door open, look out the window, and see him hoofin' out past the stables to the garage. He's carrying one of those humongous gym bags, and the Mick's kinda tucked into his jacket. Like you might carry a baby, y'know?"

"And that's when you saw him ride off," I said with a nod.

"On Doc Pilsner's scooter, yeah. Or whatever you call that thing she used to buzz around in when she'd feed those stray cats around town—"

"A Vespa," I said, picturing her on it. She'd made those rounds every night, winter or summer.

"Do you know which way Orlando went?" Vaughn said.

"Started out toward town," Bry said with another stiff little shrug. "But then he hung a left around the corner. Could 'a gone anywhere from there. I ran out to take a look but didn't see him. He was really zoomin'."

I took a deep breath. "What did you do next, Bry?"

"Broke out my cell right there on the street," he

said. "I was on my way back to the house when I phoned you."

"And you never thought to contact the police?" Vaughn said.

From the incredulous look Bry gave him, you'd have thought Vaughn had asked whether he'd considered dialing Superman's Fortress of Solitude.

"When in doubt call Skyster. That's my motto," Bry said. "I—" He broke off, cocked his head toward the front of the house. "You hear that?"

I shook my head no. "Hear what?"

"I dunno . . . sounded like somebody got into a car out front."

I realized I had noticed something like that. But I'd been concentrating on Bry's story and was mainly concerned with the sort of cars that would arrive blaring police sirens.

Vaughn quickly stepped out into the foyer, returned. "I didn't see anyone. And the only vehicles in front of the house belong to the two of you." He shrugged. "It must have been a neighbor."

Though his explanation was good enough for me, I could tell it didn't do too much to settle Bry's nerves. But his jumpiness was understandable. The momentary diversion had said everything about the serious trouble Orlando was in—and our pressing need to figure out what to do about it.

I glanced down near the foot of the sofa, where his electronic tracker lay discarded at the edge of a large Persian rug. The bracelet was bent and pulled apart as if he'd used pliers to clip it off his ankle.

"The police won't take long to show up," I said.

"No, they won't," Vaughn said. "At the bail hearing it was explained that an alarm sounds at the Middleton correctional facility. They then notify the local authorities."

I nodded. "It's probably best to let them handle this mess. Bry can fill them in—"

"Removing a police monitoring device is a felony," Vaughn interrupted. "Orlando's bail will be revoked and he'll be back in prison."

He was right, and I felt terrible about that. But Orlando had known what he was doing.

"He fled house arrest," I said. "You can't protect him from the consequences."

"Sky, please hear me out," Vaughn said, shaking his head. "I'm convinced Orlando wouldn't have done it without some desperate reason. The district attorney has already started building a case that he killed Gail. This will only substantiate it . . . unless I can show his intention wasn't to escape trial."

"Do you have any idea what it was?"

"No," Vaughn said. "I only wish."

"Have you informed the DA that Gail was Orlando's mother?"

He shook his head. "Not yet."

"Why?"

He didn't answer. His silence said everything, though.

"You expected me to leak the story to the *Anchor*, didn't you?" I said. "That's how come you told it to me in the first place."

Vaughn looked at me. I looked pointedly back. Skiball mewled in her carrier as if to second my indignation.

"As an investment counselor, I always dealt in calculated moves," he said. "My thought was that the public should learn of it first. That it might put pressure on the prosecution even while they formulated their case."

"And you were under the impression I'd be all too eager to jump at a scoop. Being a lowly small-town columnist trying to go big-time."

"It was a mistake," he said. "I sincerely apologize."

I pressed my lips together, pouched my cheeks

with air, and slowly blew it out. I didn't like knowing Vaughn tried to manipulate me. I liked it less that he'd automatically taken me for an opportunist. But I believed he was being truthful about his motives and that made it easier to understand.

"Skyster," Bryan said. "There're a couple things I scoped in the clinic. I mean, stuff that makes my brain go ooga-ooga. I want the two 'a you to see them before the cops get here."

I nodded and carefully set Skiball's carrier down on the sofa. A moment later we followed Bry out into the entry foyer, through the door to the veterinary offices, and then back to a large floor cabinet in the kennel area.

"This's the pantry," he said. "Take a look inside."

He opened the pantry's door and I saw that it was filled with ten-pound bags of puppy food—the same high-end brand I fed Ski.

"Gail ran a boarding kennel," I said. "What's so odd about her stocking up on puppy food?"

"I been comin' here to clean twice a week, Skyster," Bry said. "She'd always tell people to bring their own dog food. When you change it all of a sudden, it can give poochie stomach problems. Plus the doc wasn't even boarding any puppies."

"You're positive?"

"Trust me, I oughta know," Bry said. "Cleanin' the kennels was my job. You're lookin' at a human pooper-scooper."

I left that alone, thinking Bry had a point about all that expensive puppy food. There must have been twenty bags in the pantry. But hadn't a neighbor told the police she'd heard dogs on the night of the murder? Plural?

"All right, Bry. What else?" I said. "You mentioned a couple of unusual things."

He motioned for Vaughn and me to stay put, hurried out into an adjacent examining room, and returned after a second with a folded sheet of bright pink copy paper.

"This was behind one of those cabinets with medical whatnots on 'em . . . looked like it must've slipped behind it," he said. "Turns up while I'm cleanin' the floor this morning, and I put it away in a drawer. Don't know what it means, or if it's really too important, but I was gonna tell you about it anyway."

I unfolded the sheet of paper and my eyes widened. It was a recent La Dee Das recital program—or a photocopy of one—featuring the names of the vocal group's dozen or so members. Five of the names had check marks beside them, including Natalie Oswald and Chloe Edwards.

Scribbled atop the list was a single word: *perritos.*

Staring down at the program, I recalled the conversation I'd had with Kimi Fosette back on Abbott Lane not half an hour earlier.

"You heard a dog in Nat's house?"

"Yes."

"A barking dog?"

"No. Not barking. I suppose you'd call it yelping. Like a puppy. But the sound was clearly coming from Natalie's windows. The most bewildering thing is that she didn't own a dog."

I thought about Kimi's remarks. I thought about the neighbor's testimony. Then I read over those checkmarked names on the program.

The names, and the word penned above them.

Perritos. It was Spanish for "puppies."

Though I couldn't have explained why, not quite, the program was suddenly shaking in my hand.

Chapter 18

I could hear patrol car sirens shrieking from the direction of Main Street as Bryan and I raced from the Pilsner house to our parked vehicles—I'd pulled my Versa right behind his Ford Fairmont beater when I got there minutes before.

"You mind if I ask what you're thinking before we split up?" Bry said.

It was a fair question. The problem was that I didn't have an answer. My gut told me there was a connection between puppies, murder, Chloe's secretive activities, and Orlando skipping out on house arrest. But I couldn't have said what it might be if my life had depended on it.

Edgily aware of the police sirens, I got out the Versa's remote key fob, then realized I'd left its doors unlocked. *As if nothing bad ever happens in the Cove.* I supposed I was as lax about it as most.

I put Skiball's carrier in the front seat, and then scanned the La Dee Das program in my hand. The three checked names besides Chloe's and Nat's were "Ruth Ginken," "Jackie Sutter," and "Robynn Varriano."

"I'm sort of winging it," I said. "Haven't had a chance to think."

"Nothin' wrong with that," Bry said. "It's my personal creed."

I reached up and ruffled his spiky hair.

"You have your list?" I'd made two second-generation Xeroxes of the program on a copier in Gail's office and given him one.

"Right here." Bry patted a zippered side pocket of his biker jacket, then exchanged an apprehensive glance with me. The sirens were very close now.

"The Fog Bell's my first stop," I said. "I want to see if Chloe's around. And I'd better let Ski out of her carrier—she's ready for a claustrophobic meltdown."

He nodded. "Where to? For me, I mean."

"Jackie's in Lanesville. She should be first. Then Robynn's place in Annisquam . . . That way you can swing round the Cape without doubling back," I said. "You're positive you can find them?"

Bry gave another nod. He'd used his cell phone's wireless Internet connection to white page and Google map their addresses and directions.

"Ruth's farmhouse is right in town, so I'll head there after the inn," I said. "Stay in touch over the phone, okay?"

"Right."

"And keep your eyes and ears open for Orlando."

"Uh-huh."

"And puppies."

"Uh-huh, uh-huh."

"And anyone or anything that looks like trouble."

"Uh-uh, uh-huh, uh-huh."

I looked at him and felt a tremendous swell of affection. "Bry, I don't know what I'd do without you."

He shrugged. "Maybe, like, twice your share of the cleaning?"

A flit of a smile, and then I went around to my driver's door.

"Skyster?"

I paused halfway inside the Versa. Bry had already raced ahead to his car and was looking back at me.

"Careful," he said, and turned his key in the door.

I nodded and we drove off in separate directions, Bry turning north toward Route 127, while I went south toward the Fog Bell. With almost no traffic on Main Street, it was all I could do keep from pouring on the gas. It also wasn't ten seconds later that I saw two police cars shoot toward and then past me in the opposite lane. Sirens howling, roof bars flashing, they were plainly headed for the Pilsner home.

I whewed in relief, glad I'd held my speed down to the fifteen-miles-per-hour town limit. The last thing I wanted was to draw their attention.

Chloe's Beetle was in the garage when I got to the Fog Bell. About as glad to see it as I'd ever been, I parked just up from the garage on Carriage Lane, slid out of my seat, and went around to fetch Ski.

As I reached in for her cat carrier, I noticed a crumpled tissue sticking partly out from under the passenger seat. I bent, picked it up, frowned. I'd been going through Kleenex in bunches lately because of my runny nose. But I kept the Versa neat-freak clean. A tissue—or any litter—on the floor was like snow in July. Plus, I couldn't figure out what it was doing on the passenger side. Though with all my rushing around over the past couple of days, and bringing Ski in and out on vet runs besides, I supposed I might have dropped it there without spotting it.

Shrugging, I tossed it in the nylon waste bag strapped to the back of my seat. Then I grabbed Ski's carrier, went in the Fog Bell's entrance, and knocked on Chloe's door.

No answer. I knocked again, waited. Nobody came to the door. I *did* hear Oscar wearing out a clarinet reed in his studio, not that he'd ever bother interrupting a practice session to acknowledge visitors or answer the phone.

Maybe Chloe had gone on some nearby errands, I thought. She typically walked to the bank and post office, since they were just a few blocks away.

Then it struck me that if she'd stepped out of the house, she certainly hadn't heard about Nat. If she had heard, routine deposits and mailings would have been the last things to concern her. And because she steadfastly refused to use a cell phone, none of her friends who might know of what had happened could reach her after she left.

I hoped she wouldn't get wind of it through the town grapevine while she was running her everyday rounds. That would be a tough way to be hit with the news.

With that unsettling thought in mind, I was about to hasten upstairs to drop off Ski when I heard a low whistling sound inside the house. I held up at the bottom of the stairs, listening.

A teapot. Oscar had put water up to boil.

All swell and wonderful, except Oscar never boiled water or anything else when he had his head in a cloud of musical notes. Chloe had banned it because he'd forgotten about whatever he put on the stove way too often, scalding pots and kettles, and once almost setting the whole house on fire.

I listened some more as the whistling grew louder and louder in shrill discord with Oscar's melodic strains.

I opened the door a crack. "Chloe?" I said. "You home?"

Nothing but the steady whistle of the teapot and Oscar playing his clarinet back in the parlor. I poked my head in. "Chloe?"

Wheeeeeeeee . . .

Carrying Ski with me, I went through the door into the foyer. Chloe's laundry room was to my immediate right, with the kitchen beyond it. I paused by the washer and dryer, looked through the open kitchen entry. The steam spouting from the kettle had started to fog the room and windows.

Wheeeeeeeee . . .

I went quickly over to the stove, turned off the flame, and transferred the kettle to a cool burner. It took a while for the whistling to peter out—that water had really been going.

This was just too strange. Chloe definitely wasn't around, but it was unthinkable that she'd carelessly leave the house with the water on . . . under normal circumstances. And although I figured it was probably a waste to ask Oscar if he knew where she was—Oscar barely knew where *he* was half the time—I decided I ought to give it a shot in light of what had happened to Nat.

I was starting for the parlor when two things caught my eye, one beside the other: a hastily scribbled note on the side counter, and the blinking number one on the cordless wall phone and answering-machine combo above it.

The note, written in Chloe's handwriting, read:

Oscar,
Had to rush out to an emergency La Dee Das re-
hearsal! Be back late. Lunch is in fridge!
XXX
Chloe

I stood staring at it for a moment. An emergency La Dee Das rehearsal? What was that supposed to mean?

Too, too strange. More than that, it puzzled and worried me.

My eyes jumped to the blinking number one on the message indicator. Would it be wrong to play it back? Letting yourself into someone else's house and listening to her voice messages were bedrock don't-dos.

"Under normal circumstances" again being the operative phrase.

I jabbed the playback button and listened.

"Chloe . . . it's Jackie. I'm guessing you've already left. I just wanted you to know the boy's been here. He's on a scooter with a monkey and is on his way over to Robynn's. I called her and she's okay, thank God. I'm fine too. I'll be waiting for you and Skip outside the house."

Jackie hung up without a good-bye.

I stood thinking. There it was. Chloe and her

fellow songbirds were obviously mixed up in whatever was going on with Orlando. But what *was* going on? And who was Skip? The message possibly raised as many questions as it answered . . . but it had answered a lot.

I inhaled, exhaled, trying to decide on my next step. In his parlor, Oscar blew something jazzy. *Let him be,* I thought. Chloe'd had her reasons for keeping him in the dark about whatever she was involved in. Probably because she had known he'd be no help. Unless woodwind accompaniment was beneficial.

I pulled my cell out of my bag and speed-dialed Bry.

"Yo, Skyster," he answered. "We must be on the same psychic freq; I was about to call you—"

"Where are you, Bry?"

"In Lanesville. At Jackie Whatsername's digs. But it doesn't look like anybody's home."

"If you don't see Jackie out front, she's probably left," I said. "Go on ahead to Robynn Varriano's house. If nobody's there, call me. Right away, okay?"

"Okay." Bry hesitated. "What's up at your end? Sounds like you're in a Code Red."

"I'll explain later," I said. "I have to ditch Ski so I can get to Ruth Ginken's. And in a hurry."

Chapter 19

The widow of a nationally renowned painter of rustic oils, Ruth Ginken lived in a restored brown-shingle farmhouse at Murphy's Bend, a semi-countrified corner of town about three-quarters of a mile from the Fog Bell. The place was on more than two acres of land bordered by one of the Cove's abandoned granite quarries, making it fairly isolated, and allowing me to drive there in just a few minutes on a treelined road that was free of any traffic.

I'd come to within ten or twenty yards of Ruth's private drive when I glimpsed the familiar black Lexus through the trees to my right, heading up the drive toward the road ahead. It was bumping along at a decent clip when it reached the turnoff and took a sharp left into the oncoming lane.

Within seconds it had gotten close enough for me to see the occupants in front through its windshield. The silver-haired man was driving, surprise, surprise. Beside him in the passenger seat, Chloe resembled a fugitive from a cricket match—or maybe the Kentucky Derby—in enormous dark sunglasses and a floppy, wide-brimmed sun hat. Though I couldn't make out the faces of the women in the crowded backseat, I had no doubt they were Ruth, Jackie, and Robynn of La Dee Das fame.

As the Lexus approached, I honked my horn to catch the attention of Chloe and her friend behind the wheel—not that I should've needed to do that. Aside from ours being the only two cars on the road, Chloe would have recognized my Versa. She had to be able to see me as well as I could see her. Better, because I didn't have a hat the size of the RMS *Queen Elizabeth* on my head.

Instead of slowing, the Lexus sped up. When it momentarily came alongside me, Chloe and I looked at each other through our windows in a virtual replay of our last drive-by. I didn't know what sort of reaction to expect this time around.

But it wasn't seeing her scrunch down in her seat and push her hat down almost to her eyebrows, which was precisely what she did.

And then they all went shooting down the road in the direction I'd just come from. What the heck?

I went on to Ruth's drive, backed slightly in, U-turned, and raced on after them. I was unconcerned with town speed limits or the police now. All I cared about was getting to the bottom of things.

It didn't take long before I'd caught up to the Lexus. Barely a car length behind it, I hit the horn again. The silver-haired man kept going steadily forward. I honked a third time. He didn't slow.

That was it. With no vehicles in sight in the opposite lane, I swung my wheel to the left passed the Lexus, and cut in front of it. I kept going at a fair clip until I'd pulled what I thought would be a safe distance ahead, and then tapped my brake pedal, keeping my eyes on the Lexus in my rearview.

I had assumed the silver-haired man would be watching my brake lights. Mistake. Whatever he was watching, my rear lights weren't in the picture, and his front fender bumped my tail end hard enough to whip me forward in my seat and send the Versa into a brief skid. If I hadn't been strapped in, my head would have bashed against the dash and the situation would have gotten very ugly—though I wouldn't have been in any condition to know about it. Or anything else. For a while or maybe forever.

My tires screeched as I somehow kept my wits about me, got control of the Versa, and bounced to a stop on the road's gravel shoulder, my right bumper grazing a tree for an added jolt. Then, next thing I knew, the Lexus had veered to an abrupt halt on the shoulder ahead of me. Its doors flung open and everyone came pouring out and rushing over, the driver and Chloe leading the pack.

"Oh no! Oh my!" I could hear Chloe yelling outside my window as she jerked on my door handle. "Sky, are you all right? Answer me, please! Please, dear, *please, please answ*—"

Shaken up but otherwise intact, I fingered the button to unlock the door. Chloe hauled it open with such force that she stumbled back into the silver-haired man, her floppy hat tipping sideways to hang by its chin strap.

"Chloe, will you cool out?" I looked out at her. "You're being a total flake."

She pushed forward again and threw her arms around me, her hat still askew.

"Sky . . . what have I done?"

"You mean besides almost kill both of us?"

I suddenly wished I hadn't said that. Not because Chloe didn't deserve it, but because it made her tighten her hold on me so I could hardly breathe. She was crying hard, her cheek pressed wetly against mine.

"Sky, forgive me. I only meant to protect you," she sobbed. "You're my best friend. It's easier to forgive an enemy than to forgive a friend. I think Henry Thoreau said it. At first I didn't understand. But then I realized it's because we expect terrible things from enemies. I'd *never* want to kill my friend—"

"Chloe."

"Yes?"

"I appreciate the hug and Thoreau quote. But you're choking me while you babble," I said. "How about letting me unhook my seat belt?"

She loosened her grip enough for me to do that.

"Are you all right, young lady?" This was from the silver-haired man, who stood peering down at me from over her shoulder. "I think I should call an ambulance."

I shook my head. "No, I don't need one."

"Are you certain? I accept full responsibility and will cover any medical expenses—"

"Seriously," I said. "I'm good."

"What about your vehicle? If you need body-work or other repairs . . . ?"

"We can worry about it later," I said. "I think I just scraped that tree. Don't think there's more than a dent in my side."

He swallowed with relief, offered his hand. "My deepest apology, then," he said. "I've waited months to meet you, Sky. My name is Skip Averil. You may have heard of the Bayside Inn? I operate it with my life partner, Davies Kearns. It's quite elegant, though we do try to be reasonably affordable."

We shook. Only in the Cove will somebody make a long-winded introduction and pitch their B&B all within three minutes after driving you off the road.

Shrugging free of my seat belt, I shifted around, swung my legs out the door, and sat looking up at Chloe, Skip, and the three worried-looking women who'd been riding in the Lexus's backseat.

"I need you to tell me what's been going on," I said to Chloe.

She looked at me. "Sky . . . did you hear about Natalie?"

I nodded yes. "I'm sorry, Chloe."

"It's dreadful," she said in a moist, sorrowful voice. "After Gail, and then Nat . . . we knew we couldn't put anyone else in jeopardy with the rest of us."

"In jeopardy of what?" I said. "Chloe, I have to know—"

"It's about the rotties," Jackie said.

Chloe gave her a reproachful glance. "Shhh. You shouldn't have said anything."

"Rotties?" I said. "What're rotties?"

They all stared at me in silence.

"Is somebody here going to speak up?" I demanded. "For instance, you, Chloe?"

She turned back to face me, saw my serious expression, and finally expelled a relenting sigh.

"Rottweilers," she said. "There are five puppies. Gail rescued them from a dogfighting ring in Lowell."

"One of its leaders brought a wounded dog to her a while ago, thinking a small-town veterinarian wouldn't figure out how it had gotten hurt," Skip said. "When she recognized it was mauled in a fight, she secretly began gathering information on their operation. Orlando even pretended to be interested in betting on the fights . . . They never knew he was Gail's son."

"And the puppies . . . ?"

"They're champion stock dogs," Skip said. "The ringleader brought their mother to Gail when she was ready to give birth to the litter. I suppose he wanted to avoid veterinarians in his area."

I took a second to digest that, nodded. Everything was coming together for me, the puzzle pieces falling into place. I'd read that dogfighting was an epidemic problem in Lowell's inner-city neighborhoods, where it had become part of the gang scene. The breeders there must have been concerned that a local vet could be working with city cops to bust their operation. So they went up the road to Pigeon Cove, figuring they'd find a bumpkin who'd see no evil and ask no questions.

"Gail outsmarted them and kept the puppies," I said.

"They stayed with us," Chloe said with a nod. "I offered to hide the first, but was afraid you might figure things out if I brought my puppy to the Fog Bell."

"What would've been wrong with that, Chloe?"

She looked at me. "You've been through so much since moving to the Cove," she said. "Abe Monahan's murder. Then Kyle Fipps, the piping incident last winter, and the rest . . . I felt you needed to be spared any more excitement for a while. So I asked Davies—he plays piano and is the opening act at some of our recitals—if he and Skip could care for one rotty. Then I spoke to Nat, who took the second. Jackie, Robynn, and Ruth here volunteered to care for the rest."

"How'd the breeders find out where they were being kept?" I said. "The program with your names on it was still at Gail's office today when—" I stopped. "She had two of them. The original and a copy for Orlando."

Skip was nodding. "I believe Orlando was able to quickly put his list out of sight when they broke into Gail's office . . ."

By slipping it behind a cabinet, I thought.

". . . but they must have gotten hold of Gail's when they ransacked the place," Skip said. "They used it to find Natalie."

"And now she's dead and they have her puppy," I said.

He nodded soberly.

I was quiet for a second, trying to process everything. "I don't understand why Orlando didn't tell this to the police," I said.

"He planned to," Skip said. "*Plans* to. Today."

I looked at him.

"Orlando couldn't reveal the truth until he was convinced the puppies were safe," he said. "And he wouldn't feel that way while Gail's killers were still at large searching for them. Not unless he actually had the puppies in his hands."

I wasn't simply looking at Skip now. I was staring.

"That's why he escaped house arrest," I said. "To gather the rotties in one place before the breeders could get hold of them."

Jackie was nodding. "He came by our homes to pick them up this morning," she said.

"On Gail's Vespa."

She nodded some more.

"And where are Orlando and the puppies now?"

"At the Bayside with Davies, where the brutes that killed Gail and Nat will never know to look for them," Skip said. "Once we're all there to help him explain things, he intends to surrender to Chief Vega."

I took a deep breath, pulled my legs back through my door.

"What are you doing, dear?" Chloe said. "You really shouldn't be driving right now."

"I must agree," Skip said. "Not after you were hit—"

I made a slicing gesture with my hand. "Any of you speak Spanish well enough to translate for Orlando?"

They all looked at me in silence.

"Then lead the way," I said, and shut my door.

Chapter 20

Orlando and I were kneeling on the floor of Skip and Davies's downstairs study, Mickey on his shoulders, the gym bag full of black and rust Rottweiler puppies between us.

"They're so tiny," I said.

"*Sí, son pequeñitos.*"

"And sweet."

"*Sí, dulces también.*"

"Gentle too!"

"*Muy, muy afectuosas,*" Orlando agreed with a nod.

I looked down at the puppies. So did Orlando and Mickey. None was much larger than Skiball. I didn't understand why that had surprised me. But then, their playful, affectionate dispositions had also come as a surprise when I should have known better. Rottweilers were working dogs. The ones that became fighters weren't born vicious. Warped, vicious people made them that way.

"Excuse me, Orlando," I said after a moment. "But who's translating for whom around here?"

He smiled, but I could see the sadness in his eyes.

"Gail . . . my mother . . . she help me learn English," he said. "Now you will teach?"

I gave him a nod, softly placed a hand on his arm. "Yes," I said. "I'll be very happy to teach you."

"Sky! Orlando?"

I turned toward the doorless entryway, saw Chloe leaning her head into the woody, book-lined room.

"Yes?" I said.

"Davies has fixed us a delightful lunch in the back parlor," she said. "The two of you—well, three of you, since he does have fruit for Mickey—won't want to miss it."

I glanced at my watch. "Be with you soon, Chloe. Chief Vega ought to show up any minute and I want to let him in."

She nodded. "We'll wait until he can join us," she said, and retreated.

Orlando was silent a moment. I could tell he was struggling to translate his thoughts into English for me. *"El jefe de la policía* . . . Chief Vega . . . you say he will believe all I tell him, yes?"

It was my turn to smile.

"These cuties are pretty strong proof you're giving him the truth," I said, motioning at the puppies. *"Son las pruebas."*

He nodded. More silence. Again, though, it was easy to read his emotions in those large, expressive brown eyes. And this time they showed intense trepidation.

"I already spoke with Chief Vega over the phone," I said. *"Confía en él.* Trust him. He'll do everything possible to find the men who killed your mother and Natalie. The puppy they took from Nat's home too. Vega is my friend and a good man. When he gets here—"

We heard the resonant chime of an old brass bell at the front door.

"Right on cue," I said. "I'll answer . . ."

Orlando shook his head. "I am a man," he said. *"No soy muchacho."* He sprang to his feet, Mickey still perched comfortably on his shoulders. "Before, I run and run from police. But now I do not run."

I nodded. Vega wouldn't figure he was running. But it wasn't about that. Orlando needed to prove something to himself more than anyone else.

He walked out to the front door and opened it. There was a side porch off the study, and I drifted over to it while I waited, craning my head to try to spot Vega's cruiser through its multipaneled French doors.

But the car that had pulled up wasn't a police cruiser. In fact, it wasn't even a car. It was a white Grand Cherokee on a raised suspension with big whitewall tires. I could see the men who'd gotten out of it from where I stood, and was ready to vouch that they weren't early-season guests at the B&B coming to take in the brisk ocean air.

My pulse sped up. I knew who they were. I knew they'd come for the pups. What I didn't understand was how they could have found them.

All in their mid-twenties, they wore loose, low-riding pants and head scarves, and sported loads of diamond-crusted bling. I glimpsed one with long, dreadlock braids spilling over a waist-length black jacket with a huge painted death's-head in front, and a smaller skull and crossbones on each shoulder.

Another had on a denim jacket with raggedly cutoff sleeves over a purple hoodie. If they were going for the stereotypical cholo look, they'd done a great job of it. But the mentality of hoodlums who hunted in packs made them conformists to the bone.

One more thing I noticed about this bunch: They'd pulled handguns out from under their saggy clothes. Which said to me that their particular brand of conformity made them very dangerous.

I briefly considered lunging into the parlor for help, but dismissed the thought in a heartbeat. What were the La Dee Das supposed to do? *Sing* those creeps away?

And then I heard Orlando shouting from the door, "Sky! *¡Tome los perritos! ¡Necesitas salir! ¡Corre!*"

I wouldn't have needed to know a single word of Spanish to realize he wanted me to take the puppies and run. And if I still hadn't understood, Mickey's piercing, frantic screech would have tipped me off.

I hurried over to the gym bag and tried zipping it shut, but the rotties kept popping their heads out as though it were some kind of new, fun game. I pushed one in, and another appeared. I pushed that one down, and up came two more floppy-eared heads.

"C'mon, guys," I whispered, trying to get them back inside. "Not *now*."

The rotties stared at me curiously but weren't ready to stop playing. A tongue slurped my wrist. Somebody nibbled on my jacket sleeve. One yelped mischievously and tried climbing out for a romp before I managed to get him all the way back into the bag.

Finally I gave up. It would have to be half-zipped or nothing. Grabbing the bag's strap, I hefted it off the floor and bolted out the side of the house through the French doors.

I stood out on the porch, glanced this way and that. The Cherokee was over to my right. I saw nothing but woods to the left. The waterfront—and apparent reason Skip and Davies named their B&B the Bayside Inn—was directly ahead of me down a broad and gradually sloping lawn.

After a moment I saw something else. Actually, two identical somethings.

A pair of motorboats was docked at the bottom of the slope. Small fiberglass boats with outboard engines. Though everyone in the Cove was still too busy coughing and sneezing to think about sailing, it *was* technically spring, and I assumed the innkeepers must have recently pulled them from their winter berths.

I stood there trying to decide if—

"*¡Ella está alla!*" a male voice shouted. Meaning "She's over there!"

Since it hadn't been Orlando yelling at the top of his lungs, and since I seemed to be the only "she" around, my decision suddenly became very easy.

This despite the fact that I'd never piloted a boat, motorized or otherwise, in my life. Unless you counted rowing in Central Park.

I went bounding over the porch steps and down the slope at an all-out run. Over my right shoulder, I saw the guy with the skull jacket whirl away from Orlando and start after me. But even as he did, Mickey reached out over Orlando's head with both paws, grabbed his dread braids, and yanked.

Judging from Skull Jacket's high-pitched scream of pain, it was evident the Mick had pulled very hard. And judging by the way his pistol-toting *compañeros* froze where they stood, they wanted no part of a seemingly crazed monkey.

I scrambled down the lawn, Orlando's gym bag full of puppies swinging in my right hand. I'd heard more shouted exchanges in Spanish behind me—it sounded as if Skull Jacket had somehow freed his hair extensions from Mickey and ordered his posse back on track.

I fought the urge to shoot a look over in their direction, afraid of losing even half a step. My clogged nose made it hard to breathe, so I opened my mouth wide and took in one huge gulp of air after another as I fled downhill. The rotties bounced in the bag, a few of the pups curiously poking their heads out before they went tumbling tail-over-snout back in. I strained to keep a firm grip on the bag's strap and ran toward the dock.

I was almost there—*almost*—when I heard a grunt of exertion close at my heels. This time I couldn't help but glance back over my shoulder.

It was the guy with the denim jacket and purple hoodie. Somehow, he'd just about caught up to me. There were two or three yards between us, maybe less, and that already way-too-small gap was shrinking fast.

I should also mention that he still had a gun in his hand.

I didn't panic. Panic wasn't invited to the show. Instead I remembered my hours of torture at the Get Thinner gym all winter and made like I was on a treadmill, picking up speed, my legs working rhythmically, my heart banging against my rib cage. I was trying to focus solely on the dock ahead, keep my mind on my goal and not the guy chasing after me.

The problem was that he seemed pretty aerobicized too. As fast as I was running, I hadn't put any ground between us and could still practically feel his breath on the back of my neck.

I drew in another huge mouthful of air and pushed myself ahead, cranking the imaginary treadmill underfoot to high-cal burn. The guy shouted at me, calling me a choice part of the female anatomy in vulgar Spanish. I mentally returned the insult and kept moving, moving, tramping over the grass. A few more feet and I'd reach the dock and—

And then what? How would I find a way to get into one of the motorboats before he caught me? I also very definitely hadn't forgotten about his gun. Even if I managed to outrace him, I'd be an easy target until I got the boat launched. Assuming I was even able to launch it.

I suddenly felt that unwanted and uninvited panic crashing the party again—and this time I couldn't slam the door on it. In fact, it was filling the entrance to my heart. I didn't know what to think. Didn't know what to do except run, hanging onto my desperate forward motion and a bag of bouncing, jouncing Rottweiler pups.

And so I ran. And ran some more. And had just about run onto the wooden pier when I heard a startlingly shrill cry behind me.

I chanced a second look around. I couldn't resist, having recognized the source of the cry at once.

I wasn't sure what prompted Mickey to come scrambling down the hill. Maybe he'd understood my predicament and was trying to help. Or maybe he thought the chase was some kind of fun game. I don't pretend to know how to read monkey minds, and I'll never be able to do more than guess. But whatever his reason, he'd caught up to the cholo, gotten between his legs, tripped him to the ground, and then gone bounding off somewhere to leave the guy sprawled in the grass at the shore's edge.

It was the opening I needed.

I bolted onto the dock, slung the bag into one of the boats, and hopped in after it. *Okay, what now*? I looked around. The mooring line, I thought. First things first—I needed to untie the knot.

I hastily did that, then eyed the control panel behind the boat's windscreen. There were gauges and dials, but I didn't see any kind of ignition switch. I had to figure out how to start the motor.

My eyes landed on the throttle—and the bright red button on top of the handgrip. Pushing it seemed a reasonable guess for getting the boat going.

I grabbed the lever and thumbed the button. Nothing. I pressed harder. More nothing. Okay, fine, I thought. I'd pushed hard enough. Hitting your appliances didn't make them work. I had to be doing something wrong.

My mind raced. You throttled up to go faster, throttled down to go slower. Basic throttling theory, right? And while you did all that, you steered with the wheel. Never mind that the wheel wasn't round, but shaped like a butterfly . . .

But the butterfly wheel wasn't where the red button was located. The throttle was. And that button had to have a purpose, which I was still guessing was starting the boat. So maybe the clue was in the throttling *up* part . . .

I grabbed the wheel tightly with one hand, gripped the throttle lever with my other, and pushed while simultaneously pressing the button.

The motorboat shot forward into the water with a jerk that nearly knocked me flat on my back, whipping away from shore in a flash, sheets of spray splashing over its windscreen.

I steadied myself on my feet, got both hands around the wheel. Next step for dedicated aquatic self-learners: steering. I'd steered a car. I'd steered an SUV. I'd steered a crossover vehicle. How different could it be to steer a boat? Really?

I spun the wheel toward the right and went into a wild swerving turn that made me stumble sideways, hanging on for dear life while the bag of puppies went sliding across the deck. I jerked the wheel the other way without thinking and veered sharply again, this time sending the gym bag back to the opposite side of the deck.

The shore blurred by. The boat angled precariously. I suddenly realized that I didn't know where I was relative to where I'd started out, and had no clue where I was going besides. Plus the puppies were getting banged all over the place.

I tried to look around to see if I could spot the Bayside. Or the dock. Or anything familiar that would help me find my bearings. But all that I accomplished was tipping the boat so far to one side that two of the puppies spilled out of the bag, the smallest rolling up against the inner hull of the boat like a furry bowling ball.

Clinging to the wheel with one hand, I tried to

reach for him and fell over sideways into the cold water sloshing over the deck. It soaked my clothes through and through, making them stick clammily to my skin. By now all the dogs were out of the bag, their fur so wet they resembled baby seals.

Easy, I thought, picking myself up. *Easy does it.*

I regained my hold on the wheel, took a deep breath, and this time gave it the slightest of turns to the right. The boat stabilized and went smoothly in that direction. Then I gave the wheel another slight leftward nudge. And again went pretty much where I'd intended to go without almost capsizing.

Better. Much better. I'd learned how to start a boat. Now I thought I had a clue about how to maneuver.

But I was still lost at sea. Or on the bay, as it were.

And then I heard the commotion carrying over the water from what I at least *thought* was behind me. I nudged the butterfly wheel around very slowly and gingerly, hoping the boat would go where I intended.

It did. An instant later, I saw the *tres amigos* from hell starting to pile over the gunwales of the second boat, felt a surge of panic . . . and then exhaled as that awful fear turned to pure, utter relief.

They'd been surrounded by a group of men in blue uniforms and were standing on the dock with their hands raised in the air.

I was speeding along, holding the wheel steady as I could, when I heard my cell phone Coldplay me.

I reached into my coat pocket for it.

"Sky?"

"Alex?

"We've got them," he said. "Gail and Natalie's killers."

"Alex, where are you . . . ?"

"Look behind you, Sky. At the shore."

I turned, looked, and saw him waving at me from the wooden dock.

Briefly pulling the cell phone from my ear, I waved back at him with the hand that held it, then lowered it again so I could hear him talk to me.

"Everything's okay," Vega said. "Those men are in custody and nobody's been hurt. You can turn around now."

I started to tell him I'd do just that, caught myself. "I'd love to, Alex," I said. "Only problem's it might take me a while to figure exactly how to get this thing back to shore."

That was no great disaster, though. I didn't have to hurry.

I knew Chief Alex would wait for me, however long it took.

Chapter 21

"A GPS tracker, dudette," Bry was saying. "Be kinda cool if it wasn't so uncool."

I nodded, sneezed, blew my nose. The scary thing was that I knew what he meant.

We were in my Airstream about two hours after he'd given me a lift over from the police station, where Chief Vega and his men had locked up the dogfighting crew and taken my statement. My Versa, meanwhile, was somewhere in an Essex County impound lot, where the forensic people who'd picked it over had found the global positioning unit under the dash.

"The *tres creepos* must have stuck the transmitter under my dash while were at Gail's," I said. "I'm guessing that's what you heard out front."

"That car door opening and shutting."

I nodded again. And *ah-chooed*.

"They used a tissue to clean up the smudges they left putting it in . . . Guess they used some kind of adhesive."

"And you kept the tissue."

"Tossed it in that litter bag I keep in the Versa," I said.

Bry looked down at the Rottweiler on his lap. The pup taken from Natalie Oswald's studio, it had been found in a tied laundry bag in the Cherokee that the *tres creepos* had been driving.

"So," I said. "You think of a name for our new guard dog yet?"

"I dunno." Bry shrugged. "How about Mars?"

I looked at him. "Mars?"

"Yeah. Like the planet." He scratched under her neck and she stared placidly up at him. "She seems kinda out there, y'dig?"

That one I wasn't so sure about. But since the rotty was technically his dog, I figured I would take his word.

"So anyways," Bry said, "what I want to know is why those Lowell guys didn't catch up to you at the Bayside toot sweet. I mean, if they had that GPS thing . . ."

"It got damaged when I was run into that tree near Ruth Ginken's farmhouse," I said.

"By Skip and the La Dee Das."

I nodded, thinking that sounded like the name of a second-rate sixties pop group. "Vega figures the transmitter kept turning itself off and on after the accident. Good thing too. Since that made those guys late getting there . . ."

"You mean Skull Jacket and his boys."

"Right," I said, thinking *that* sounded like a fifth-rate eighties punk-rock group. Being how we were suddenly on a naming kick. "And while it delayed them, it gave Vega and *his* boys time to catch up."

"Cavalry arrives," Bry said.

Which wasn't a good name for anything in my opinion, but you couldn't always expect to strike gold.

I dropped my used tissue in the wastebasket, reached for another, and sneezed into it.

"Want a ride home?" Bry said. "Looks to me you could use a stretch in the tub."

I nodded. We'd just stopped by to get the rotty there so it could get acclimated. "I'll get my coat and—"

My cell phone played its music and I picked it up from where I'd set it on the desk.

"Sky?"

I frowned, wishing caller ID blocking could be outlawed.

"Bill?"

"Billy to you," Drecksel said. "I was wonderin'—"

"No," I said.

"No?"

"No," I said. "I'm staying put. Right here. In my trailer."

He grunted. "You positive?"

"A hundred percent," I said, glancing at Mars. "Even have a little something to guard against bear attacks."

"What's that?"

"You'll see," I said. "Later."

Bill sighed.

"Well, you ever change your mind, let me know," he said. "If there's gotta be a tin can in my backyard, I suppose I oughtta be glad it's a neat one."

"Right, Bill." I grinned. "Notoriously neat."

That struck me as a pretty decent phrase, and I instantly slipped it into the mental file drawer where I save all my better ones.

As a professional writer and cleanup person, I had a hunch I'd find a perfect use for it someday.

SKY TAYLOR'S GRIME SOLVERS BLOG

Environmentally Conscious, Energy-Saving, Quick Steps

I'm stuffy and sniffling worse than ever tonight thanks to a cold weather motorboat ride I *really* don't want to talk about right now, so I'll be word-efficient and then climb into the sack for a good night's sleep. Of course, efficiency's this blog entry's whole point. Call it unwanted and unnecessary symmetry.

—Sky

1. Cut down on your hot water usage. Use cold or warm water for household cleaning and washing. Only white clothes need hot water washing.

2. Keep vents, heating units and light bulbs well dusted for max output. If you have pets, keeping fur from clogging up air conditioner and furnace filters is a must.

3. When you're clearing the lunch or dinner dishes, take the partially full glasses of water and pour into your house plants.

4. Save electricity and clothes-dryer time with those plastic balls you see everywhere. We don't use them exclusively, but for they're ideal for heavy loads like towels. As they bounce around, they create air pockets that speed up the drying process. Fabric softener tends to reduce the absorbency of towels and washcloths, and leaves an artificial perfumey scent that allergy sufferers can live without.

5. Usually take out the trash in the evening? Hang a battery operated light on the door of your shed or under the porch where you keep the trash cans. You'll lose an excuse to skip cleaning out those wastebaskets at the end of the day, but you'll be glad to have one less chore before heading to work in the morning.

Mother Nature's Helpers:
Outdoor Cleaning Tips

It's morning and I'm feeling lots better than yesterday. Nothing tackles a cold better than a hot bath and burrowing in under my toastiest blankets for the night. Plus the local forecast says temps in the Cove should actually scratch seventy today. Spring at last! *Zowie!*

With warm weather around the corner, and barbecues and patio parties coming to mind, here are some tips for the cleaning we have to do outdoors.

Barbecue Grills

Having to clean your gas grill just as you're about to plop on the patties can be a real hassle. It's also a gross-out when you open it to discover some freakish bug family's turned it into a country cabin. So get your cleaning done before the creepy crawlies move in.

While the grill's cool, poke away grease and

goop from the burner holes with all-purpose bamboo skewers (as my Constant Reader, you always have them handy, right?), then whisk clean with a toothbrush. We only wire-brush once, at the end of the year. Also, if you use lava rocks, flip them over from time to time so grease drippings can burn off.

Extra, extra:

If your flame is an orangey red color, it's a sign the grill has clogged burners and needs some TLC (tender loving cleaning).

Decks

Wood decks will last longer if you simply sweep away the leaves, sticks, pods, and common windblown foliage that find resting places between the boards. Think of it as mulch, in the sense that it holds moisture. That's great for garden plants, but *not* your deck, since it can cause stains and mildew.

At least once a year, wash the deck with a bucket of warm water and a long squirt of dish detergent. And every *couple* of years, call in the guys to do the power wash.

Wrought Iron

Iron fencing, gates, patio furniture, lanterns, and so forth are generally low maintenance. But they do need occasional cleaning. Scrub away rust with a wire brush, steel wool, or medium-grade sandpaper. If the birds have "dropped by," a damp cloth and soft brush will do the trick.

Patio Umbrellas

Before putting that cheerfully colored sign of summer away for the season . . . please clean it! Dirt that has accumulated on the umbrella can make for a dull, faded opening next year. In this case the fastest and easiest method for umbrella cleaning *does* belong to Mother Nature: a soaker of a rainstorm can't be beat. But from time to time, give her an assist. Just use a mild dish soap, wash, rinse, and dry.

Wicker Furniture

First, vacuum with your brush attachment. Next, using as little water as possible to avoid wood swell or rot, brush clean, sun dry, or use an electric fan to dry it off. Remember that wicker can be fickle—it needs humidity so it won't crack, but too much moisture creates mildew. And while it's fine in the sun, too much sunlight can dry it out and cause breakage. Keeping this in mind when placing your outdoor furniture will make it last a lot longer.

Windows

Everyone loves that old crumpled newspaper method . . . except me! For one thing, newspaper isn't absorbent. For another, the newsprint gets all over your hands. Do yourself a huge favor and get a squeegee for window-cleaning. It's really the drying process that creates streaks on glass, and nothing beats the rubber side of a squeegee for eliminating them.

That's it for now . . . I'm heading out to soak up some sunshine!

About the Author

Suzanne Price is the pseudonym for a national bestselling author. While Suzanne has never solved a murder, she's as quick with cleaning hints as her heroine is.

THE GRIME SOLVERS MYSTERY SERIES

FROM

SUZANNE PRICE

SCENE OF THE GRIME

In her mid-30s and recently widowed,
Sky Taylor left the big city for Pigeon Cove, a
hamlet off the Massachusetts coast. Sky is
re-adapting to single life—with a newspaper
column and her knack for creative cleaning
increasingly in demand. Then she discovers a
patron of the Millwood Inn—
permanently checked-out.

Now Sky's juggling the police chief's
questions with advances from the newest—and
handsomest—crime reporter in town. But if she
wants to clear her name, she has some
scouring to do.

Also Available
Dirty Deeds

**Available wherever books are sold or
at penguin.com**